Four Weddi
and an Elvis

A Comedy in Four Acts

by Nancy Frick

Baker's Plays
7611 Sunset Blvd.
Los Angeles, CA 90042
bakersplays.com

FOUR WEDDINGS AND AN ELVIS premiered at the Center for the Arts Community Theater (C4ACT) in Homer, New York in April 2010, under the direction of Carl Moses with the following cast:

BEV	Lori O'Donnell
STAN	Joe Cortese
SANDY	Judy Van Buskirk
JOHN	Tom Corey
LOU	Bill Sharp
VANESSA	Brenda Aulbach
BRYCE	Girish Bhat
MARVIN	Doug Walls
FIONA	Karen Moses
FIST	Matt Moses
KEN	Tom Ardis

FOUR WEDDINGS AND AN ELVIS had its second production at Old Academy Players in Philadelphia, Pennsylvania, in November 2010 under the direction of Nancy Frick, with lighting by Nicolas Burnosky and the following cast:

BEV	Bonnie Kapenstein
STAN	Joe Carney
SANDY	Chris Cutrufello
JOHN	Michael Boorse
LOU	J.P. Parrella
VANESSA	Nancy Bennett
BRYCE	Michael J. Gavanus
MARVIN	Norm Burnosky
FIONA	Brianna Tillo
FIST	Tom Owen
KEN	Mark Reichert

CHARACTERS

Bev & Stan: The Payback

    BEV – the angry bride

    STAN – the angry groom

    JOHN – the Elvis minister

    SANDY – the wedding chapel owner

Vanessa & Bryce: The Comeback

    VANESSA – the bride, a fading actress

    BRYCE – the groom, a fading actor

    LOU – the minister, 70s

    SANDY

Fiona & Marvin: The Real Thing

    FIONA – the bride, tough ex-con

    MARVIN – the groom, gentle postal worker

    FIST – scary friend of the bride

    SANDY

Sandy & Ken: The Epilogue

All characters from previous scenes will reappear in this scene. The only exception is Stan. His character will not reappear, but the actor who played him will appear as the **PRODUCER** in this scene. **KEN** will also make a brief appearance.

SETTING

All action occurs in a Las Vegas wedding chapel.

TIME

The play takes place in the present, over the span of approximately 18 months.

For Mom and Dad with love; for Mike always;
for the Old Academy and everyone who makes it so special.

Bev & Stan: The Payback

(Action takes place in a Las Vegas wedding chapel. Enter **BEV** *and* **STAN**. *They are angry.* **SANDY** *is seated at the desk reading.)*

BEV. Wow. We're here. We're really going to do it, aren't we?

STAN. You bet we are. We've flown 2,500 miles. We're not turning back now. I mean, you still want to, right?

BEV. Are you kidding me? This is gonna *kill 'em.*

STAN. It's gonna wreck 'em! Can you see their faces when we come back – married?

BEV. I'm picturing it right now.

STAN. Me too.

(They both get angry, satisfied looks on their faces.)

What do you think they're doing right now?

BEV. What time is it?

STAN. If it's ten o'clock here, it's one o'clock there. Probably having lunch.

BEV. He's making her cut the edges off his sandwich. I'll bet she never expected *that*! Real men eat the crust.

STAN. And she's serving that tuna salad she always makes. And he's pretending to like it like I did for all those years.

BEV. Well, it serves them right.

STAN. *(devious)* If they only knew what we were about to do.

BEV. It would devastate them!

STAN. It would destroy them!

BEV. I hate them for what they did to you!

STAN. I hate them for what they did to *you!*

(They are overwhelmed with anger and kiss passionately. **SANDY** *finally puts her book down and looks up. Very bored. She clears her throat to get their attention.)*

STAN. *(cont.)* Oh, hi. Sorry. We're here to, you know, do the deed. Tie the knot.

*(***SANDY*** *looks puzzled.)*

You know, get hitched. Walk down the aisle. Put on the old ball and chain.

BEV. *(enunciating each word)* We're here to get married. I don't think she speaks English.

SANDY. Oh, you want to *get married?*

(She has been playing with them. We will discover that she is definitely quirky. Maybe she's been doing this for too long.)

STAN. *(still confused)* Yes. Please.

SANDY. *(very pleasantly)* Well, we can do that. We're a wedding chapel.

STAN. I know that. That's why we're here.

SANDY. Well, good. Then we're all on the same page! Yes?

(big smile)

STAN. Yes.

BEV. Yes.

SANDY. Yes!

STAN. So, you do it right here?

SANDY. There's the altar. You're just ten steps away from wedded bliss and a lifetime of martial law! I mean marital joy. *(big quirky smile)*

STAN. I'm sorry, are you being sarcastic?

SANDY. Hmm?

STAN. Don't you think she's being sarcastic?

BEV. Maybe it's a Vegas thing.

STAN. Yeah, maybe. So, what do we need to do?

SANDY. Well, why don't you have a seat and we'll go through your options. We have a lot of different wedding packages you can choose from. Are you looking for a traditional wedding or something themed?

STAN.	**BEV.**
Traditional.	Themed.

SANDY. Okay. Our packages start at $200 and go into the thousands. Maybe we should start there. How much do you want to spend?

STAN.	**BEV.**
Two hundred.	Two thousand.

STAN. Two thousand! You really want to spend that much?

BEV. Well, it is our wedding.

SANDY. It is your wedding.

(smiles)

STAN. Yes, of course, but –

(lowering his voice to **BEV***)*

We've already spent a lot just getting here. What do we get for $200?

SANDY. *(unenthusiastically)* A rose, a boutonniere, and an 8 x 10. Don't blink!

(She takes a picture of them.)

Oh, you closed your eyes.

*(***STAN** *just doesn't know what to make of her. Then, to* **BEV***)*

STAN. Well, that's all we really need, right?

BEV. I don't know. We're here.

(to **SANDY***)*

What kind of theme weddings do you do? I've always thought it would be fun to be married by Elvis.

STAN. *(with distaste)* Really?

SANDY. We do Elvis. We do Blues Brothers. We do Wayne Newton. I think our Cher is out on maternity leave. But I could get you a Donna Summer if you want to do a disco thing. *(She sings.)* "McArthur's Park is melting in the dark…"

STAN. No, no, no. We do not want Donna Summer.

SANDY. We do Fairy Tale weddings, Victorian weddings, Gangster weddings, Star Trek weddings – in Klingon if you like – "jIH DaH maq SoH loDnal je be'nal." *(pronounced "GEE d-AH mock soCH londnal Jeh beh--nahl")* That's, "I now pronounce you husband and wife." We'll marry you on horseback, on Harleys, in a helicopter over the Grand Canyon…

BEV. Over the Grand Canyon? I always wanted to see the Grand Canyon.

(She grabs STAN's sleeve.)

Did you hear that, Stan? The Grand Canyon!

SANDY. There's the Lady of the Lake ceremony where you get married on a 60-foot private yacht.

BEV. Can we get Elvis on the yacht, too?

SANDY. Sure.

(glancing at STAN)

If he's willing to pay for it. Do you want the fat Elvis or the thin Elvis?

BEV. Oh, the thin, the thin.

SANDY. *(grabbing a brochure)* Okay, under the thin Elvis you have your choice of the army Elvis, the Hawaiian Elvis, the 1968 Comeback Elvis….

BEV. Oh, the Hawaiian Elvis! I always loved him. Will he sing, too?

SANDY. Will he sing? Whatever your little heart desires.

(flipping through brochure)

Hawaiian Elvis, Hawaiian Elvis. Here we go. Hawaiian Elvis comes with a full band, three back-up singers in grass skirts, luau pig roast, Polynesian dancers, tiki torches, fire eaters, hula lessons, flame throwers…

STAN. Whoa! Whoa! Whoa! Girls! This thing is getting way out of control! Fire eaters! Flame throwers! Fat Elviseses!

BEV. No, honey, we want the thin.

STAN. We don't want either! We just want to get married! Right now, right here! Without all of this ridiculousness.

BEV. You're calling my wedding dreams ridiculous?

STAN. These aren't your dreams! She just put them into your head! We never talked about anything like this. The plan was to come here, get married, and then go home and throw it in Ed and Jenny's faces and watch them fall apart. Remember? *That* was the dream.

BEV. Oh yeah.

STAN. Remember what they did to us? Do you remember our humiliation? How they deceived us and then divorced us?

BEV. *(more conviction)* Yeah.

STAN. How they made us look like fools!

BEV. Oh yeah!

(They are overwhelmed with anger and kiss passionately.)

SANDY. This isn't a wedding. This is a payback.

(They collect themselves.)

BEV. Okay, well, we'll just do the basic wedding.

SANDY. All right then. That's one Traditional Ceremony for the happy couple.

STAN. Okay, that! That was sarcastic!

SANDY. Hmmm?

STAN. I'm not liking your attitude.

BEV. Stan, please. Let's just do this, okay? So, when can we get married?

SANDY. *(looking at her laptop, scrolling down)* Hmmm, let's see. Thursday, Friday, Saturday –

STAN. I thought in Las Vegas you just walked in and did it.

SANDY. Yeah, you're right. There's no waiting.

(She laughs and closes the laptop.)

The only problem is my minister just stepped out for a moment.

STAN. When's he coming back?

SANDY. How long does it take to get schnockered?

(STAN looks horrified.)

Ha! Just kidding. He'll be right back. So, one Traditional Ceremony. That's a rose, a boutonniere and an 8 x 10. You know, for another $20, you can have a video of your wedding so you always remember this sacred day. Or even better, for another $50, you can broadcast it live over the Internet for family and friends who couldn't attend. Maybe you'd like to invite Ed and Jenny to watch this joyous ceremony.

STAN. Really? We can do that?

SANDY. Um hmm.

STAN. What do you think, Bev?

BEV. I think I'd better put on some lipstick! Is there somewhere I can – ?

SANDY. Sure. There's a dressing room in the back. Help yourself.

BEV. *(very excited)* We're getting married – live!

(She exits. STAN and SANDY look at each other distastefully for a moment.)

SANDY. *(big smile)* So, you must be so excited. This is your wedding day!

STAN. Aw, cut the crap.

SANDY. Thank you. It's exhausting.

STAN. Then why do you do it?

SANDY. People expect it.

STAN. Would it be too much to expect some sincerity too?

SANDY. Oh, give me a break, Stan. I've been doing this for 17 years. Can you imagine 17 years of watching people make the biggest mistake of their lives – with a big smile on my face?

STAN. You are seriously jaded.

SANDY. Twelve hours from now I'm gonna have them lined up out the door, half of them drunk, all of them "in love," whatever that means, and I'm going to have to put on my happy face and walk them down the aisle of eternal wedded bliss.

STAN. If you hate it so much, why do you do it?

SANDY. *(shrugs)* I'm a sucker for romance.

STAN. You ever been married?

SANDY. Four times. Fifth time's gonna be the charm, I can feel it. You strike me as a real romantic, too.

STAN. Yeah, right.

SANDY. Seriously, under all that anger beats the heart of a man in love.

STAN. I'm not angry.

SANDY. Yeah? And I'm not flaky.

STAN. I was only married once.

SANDY. To Jenny.

STAN. Yep.

SANDY. You got kids?

STAN. Twin boys. They live with her. With them.

(He clearly hates saying the word them.)

I see them every other weekend.

SANDY. I assume she and Ed are married now?

STAN. No. They're getting married next Saturday.

SANDY. *(with great meaning)* Aha!

STAN. What does that mean?

SANDY. It's an expression that denotes a sudden revelation.

STAN. I know what "Aha" means! What's the revelation?

SANDY. Jenny and Ed are getting married, so you're going to get married first to show them that you don't CARE that they're getting married, but the very fact that you flew thousands of miles to PROVE to them that you don't care that they're getting married says very LOUDLY how much you DO.

STAN. Do you talk to all of your customers this way?

SANDY. No, just the ones I think I can save.

(beat)

STAN. *(impatient)* How do we set up this Internet thing?

SANDY. I just give you an address and you give it to them and they watch.

STAN. Where's the camera?

SANDY. Right there.

STAN. All right. Let's do this! I'm calling Jenny.

(He pulls out his cell phone and dials.)

SANDY. You seem to know that number pretty well.

STAN. It used to be mine.

(into phone with forced bravado:)

Jenny. I thought you might be interested in watching something on the Internet. If you get this message, go to – what's the address?

SANDY. *(entering the address into her computer)* W-W-W dot little chapel dot com.

STAN. W-W-W dot little chapel dot com.

(He takes the phone from his ear, about to hang up.)

SANDY. Slash wedding broadcast slash Stan and Bev.

STAN. *(bringing the phone back up, an annoyed look at* **SANDY***)* Slash wedding broadcast slash Stan and Bev.

(taking the phone from his ear)

SANDY. Slash 2010 hypen July.

STAN. *(bringing the phone back up, more annoyance with* **SANDY***)* Slash 2010 hypen July.

(Is she done? He waits for more, than brings the phone down.)

SANDY. Slash slash slash. Dot.

STAN. *(with great irritation)* Slash slash slash. Dot!

(hanging up the phone)

Okay. Good-bye. Oh, it's Stan. Stan Dreyer.

SANDY. Okay, well, this is good. They'll watch you get married and boy will they be sorry. Right?

STAN. Right!

*(Enter **BEV** in a wedding gown. She is delighted.)*

BEV. Look what I found! There's a whole rack of them back there. Some with big hoops and parasols and puffy sleeves and slinky backs. I was going crazy trying to pick one! There's a bunch of tuxedos too.

SANDY. I see you found our rental area.

BEV. *(to **STAN**)* Yeah, I figured as long as we're doing this, and as long as they're watching, we should do it up right! Look our best. What do you think?

STAN. Yeah. Yeah. Definitely. Good idea!

BEV. Go get yourself a tux.

STAN. Yeah. We'll look so good, they're gonna eat their hearts out!

BEV. They're gonna be sick!

*(He exits. Beat. **SANDY** smiles.)*

SANDY. Well, don't you look lovely?

BEV. Stow it, crazy lady.

SANDY. Gladly.

BEV. I don't know how much longer I can keep this up.

SANDY. Keep what up?

BEV. This! All this venom. This bile. It's grueling.

SANDY. Are you saying you're not angry?

BEV. I'm not angry.

SANDY. You don't hate Jenny and Ed?

BEV. I don't hate Jenny and Ed.

SANDY. You don't want to crush 'em, or destroy 'em or otherwise do them irreparable physical and emotional harm?

BEV. No. I wish them the best. I really do.

SANDY. Well, run me over with a rented limousine. Never saw that one coming.

BEV. I do some acting back home. Community theatre. They say I was the best Blanche DuBois ever.

SANDY. Well, you're putting on quite a show today.

BEV. I know. But how do I stop? When we first found out, Stan and I were so crushed. And then we were angry. And that anger seemed to bring us together. And then at some point, I stopped being angry and started falling for Stan. And now, I just want to marry him so we can be together all the time. I'm in love.

SANDY. Yeah, but he's in hate.

BEV. I know, I know. What should I do?

SANDY. I'd start by calling off the wedding.

BEV. No. No, I can't do that. I love him. I love his scrawny arms. I love his big feet. I love his messy hair. I love his 70s wardrobe.

SANDY. You sure you don't want to set your sights a little higher?

BEV. Once we're married, everything will work out. I'm sure of it. He'll forget all about Jenny and fall in love with me.

SANDY. Do you know what I've learned after one husband, four marriages and seventeen years in this business? Any sentence that begins with "once we're married" is a train bound for heartbreak. If it ain't great now, it ain't gonna get great. And all the wishing in the world isn't going to make it so.

BEV. You're right. You're absolutely right.

SANDY. So what are you going to do?

(**STAN** *emerges in a tuxedo.*)

BEV. *(losing any resolve she may have had)* Marry the man I love.

STAN. Do I look handsome, or what?

BEV. You look wonderful.

STAN. I hope Jenn's watching! All right, let's get this show on the road. Is your minister back?

SANDY. Ummm –

STAN. Well, what's he doing? Where is he?

SANDY. That's a good question.

(Enter **JOHN***. He is dressed as Elvis. He speaks in his regular voice.)*

JOHN. Hi, Sandy. I, uh, couldn't help but notice Ken in the parking lot. He's, uh, sick. Know what I mean?

SANDY. Yeah, I know what you mean.

JOHN. I put him in the back seat of your car. He's sleeping it off.

SANDY. Thank you. Again.

STAN. Are you saying you have no minister?

SANDY. Uh, well –

(then to **JOHN***)*

You got a couple of minutes?

JOHN. *(looks at his watch)* Sure.

SANDY. Great, because this lovely couple here really wants to get married. And for all the right reasons! This is John from the wedding chapel next door and he can marry you right now. So, I'll just get your flowers and we'll be ready to go.

JOHN. I hope you don't mind getting married by Elvis. I've got a wedding at eleven that requested the King.

STAN. Doesn't matter to us. We just want to get this thing over with.

BEV. Stan! We love Elvis! This is perfect.

JOHN. Good, good. Because some people feel like it trivializes the service, you know? But I always say, hey, if you're sincere, and you're in love, it doesn't matter who marries you, right?

BEV. Right. Do you enjoy marrying people?

JOHN. Oh, yeah, it's a great gig, but –

BEV. But what?

JOHN. After marrying all these people, I kind of feel like it's my turn, you know, to meet a wonderful girl and fall in love.

(He sings the line of a love song, imitating the King.)

BEV. Oh, that's beautiful. The song and the wish. I can't believe you don't meet a lot of girls in this town.

JOHN. Oh, sure I do. But not the right kind of girls, you know. Hell, half the time, I'm not even sure they're women.

(to STAN)

We have a lot of, you know, trannies in this town.

BEV. That's a transvestite, Stan.

STAN. I know what a trannie is!

BEV. I don't think we have any of those in Virginia. We're from Roanoke.

JOHN. Oh, nice. You're just here to get married?

BEV. Yes. Marrying the man I love!

JOHN. Well, congratulations. You're a very lucky man. She's seems like a wonderful woman.

SANDY. Okay, here we go. Flowers for the blushing bride. And a boutonniere for the grimacing groom.

(She pins it on STAN.)

Now, all you need is a witness and you can enter the bonds of sweet, blissful matrimony.

STAN. *(panicked)* We don't have a witness. Nobody said anything about a witness!

SANDY. You don't have a witness! What are we gonna do? Just kidding. I'll be your witness.

STAN. Yes, fine, whatever!

(referring to the Internet camera)

Are we still live?

SANDY. Yes, we are. Elvis, take it away.

(**JOHN** *moves to the altar, grabs the microphone and uses his Elvis voice:*)

Ladies and gentlemen, live from Las Vegas, it's show time! Welcome to the wedding of two very special kids in love, uh –

SANDY. Stan and Bev.

ELVIS. Stan and Bev. Stan, bring that little lady on up here so we can celebrate your special day and your special union – Elvis style!

(*He sings a ballad as the King, then proceeds with the ceremony.*)

Now, Stan and Bev, you're *all shook up* in your love for one another. That's why we're here today. I know you've both spent some time in heartbreak hotel, we all have, but today, and every day forward, you're going to love each other tender, love each other sweet. Now, I'd like you to turn and face one another and look in each others eyes as you hold hands. Bev, will you have Stan to be your husband? Will you love him and comfort him, honor and keep him, and forsaking all others, forever be his hunk-a-hunk-of-burning-love?

BEV. I will.

ELVIS. Stan, will you have Bev to be your wife? Will you love and comfort her –

(**STAN**'s *cell phone rings.*)

Honor and keep her, and forsaking all others, forever be her hunk-a-hunk-of-burning-love?

(*It continues to ring.*)

STAN. I'm sorry.

BEV. You're not going to get that, are you?

STAN. It might be important.

BEV. We're getting married, Stan!

ELVIS. I gotta agree with the little lady. If you answer that –

   (He sings.)

   "You ain't nothing but a hound dog…"

STAN. *(answering phone)* Hello? Hello? Who? I can't hear you.

   (to **ELVIS***)*

   Do you MIND?

   *(***ELVIS** *stops singing.* **STAN** *listens for a several moments, then takes the phone away from his ear.)*

BEV. Well? Who is it? What do they want?

STAN. It's Jenny. She's watching. She said don't do it.

BEV. What?

STAN. She said don't do it. Don't get married.

BEV. How dare she? She ruins our lives once and that's not enough? She's gotta do it again?

   (Remembering the camera, she speaks directly to it.)

   Once wasn't enough, Jenny? You gotta try and spoil my happiness a second time? Well, bring it on, bitch! Bring it on! Is she still on there? Give me the phone. Give me that phone! Give-it-to-me!

   (She struggles with **STAN***, and eventually gets the phone as he falls to the ground.)*

ELVIS. The river of love runs a mighty crooked course.

BEV. *(into phone)* It's Beverly. What the hell do you think you're doing? What?! You what? This is insane. I'm losing my mind. Elvis. I think I may faint.

   *(***ELVIS** *steps in to support her as she goes weak.)*

STAN. Are you all right?

BEV. Yes.

STAN. Good.

   (He takes the phone.)

   It's me again. Do you really? What about him? When? Are you saying that you want me back?

BEV. Stan, hang up the phone. Right now! Elvis, pick up where you left off. I think we were at hunk-a-hunk-of-burning-love. Come on, Stan. Stand next to me.

(prompting **ELVIS***)*

Elvis, come on! It's now or never!

ELVIS. *(confused, he sings)* "It's now or never, come hold me tight…"

BEV. What are you doing?!

ELVIS. I thought you wanted me to sing, darlin'.

BEV. No, I want you to hurry up!

STAN. Stop, Bev, just stop. It's no use. I'm still in love with Jenny. And it seems, she still loves me, too.

BEV. No, no, if you just hang up everything will be okay. Once we're married, everything's going to work out fine.

SANDY. I tried to tell her where that train goes.

STAN. I'm sorry. I don't love you. I love Jenn. I've always loved Jenn.

(to the camera)

I'm coming home, baby! I'm taking the first plane! I love you, I love you, I love you!

ELVIS. Stan, don't be cruel.

STAN. *(to* **BEV***)* I'm sorry. But we were just getting even. It wasn't like we were in love or anything, right?

BEV. Right.

STAN. *(to the camera)* Tell the boys Daddy's on his way home!

(He exits, singing.)

"Viva, Las Vegas!"

SANDY. Hey! Hey! Wait!

(She runs after him to the door.)

BEV. Don't try to stop him.

SANDY. He's wearing my best Armani! He's gone.

BEV. *(to* **SANDY***)* Well, I guess you got your wish.

SANDY. This isn't what I wished for. Not like this.

ELVIS. I know things look pretty bleak, little lady, but you know what Elvis always says? "When things go wrong, don't go with them."

BEV. Elvis, do you mind if I talk to John?

JOHN. I'm here.

BEV. What am I supposed to do now?

JOHN. I guess you feel bad for awhile, until you don't feel bad any more, and then you hope to meet someone new.

BEV. How long will that take?

JOHN. The feeling bad part? I don't know. But you meet new people all the time. Hi, I'm John.

BEV. I'm Bev.

SANDY. Oh dear.

(They shake hands and smile. **SANDY** *shakes her head as the curtain closes.)*

Vanessa & Bryce: The Comeback

(Months later. SANDY enters from the back with a vase of flowers. The phone rings. She answers.)

SANDY. Coming! Coming! Sandy's Chapel of Love. Oh hi, John. – Yes, I'm all set, thanks. I talked to someone last night who sounds perfect. He's worked in Vegas for years, done lots of ceremonies – yes, he does Elvis, too, which is great. So I'm not going to have to impose on you any more. – No, Ken's still gone. On a real bender this time, I guess. – Yeah, I know, I know. I'll tell you, John, if he wasn't my husband, he'd be so fired.

(A little old man walks in the door.)

I've got customers. Gotta go. – And, John, thanks for checking on me. – Okay, bye.

(to man)

Good morning. Are you with the Wells-Cannon party?

LOU. No, I'm here for the minister job.

(SANDY looks confused.)

We talked last night. I'm Lou DeGeorge. How do you do?

SANDY. You're Lou?

LOU. Yeah, I hope I'm not too early, but you said you had a wedding at 11:00 and I didn't want to be late. Nice chapel.

SANDY. You're Lou? Lou, who said on the phone that he can play Elvis?

LOU. That's right.

SANDY. *You* do Elvis?

LOU. Of course. I've been playing Elvis for 40 years. In fact, I was one of the very first Elvis impersonators on the Strip.

SANDY. That I believe.

LOU. Here, listen…

(He sings as the King.)

SANDY. That was terrible.

LOU. Well, it's early. I'm not warmed up. I'm not wearing my sideburns. I'm – I'm –

SANDY. At least 70 years old!

LOU. What, so that disqualifies me? This is age discrimination. You were much nicer on the phone last night.

SANDY. And you were much younger. Look, for most weddings, I don't care how old you are. But I was really hoping to hire someone who could do *all* my weddings, Elvis and non-Elvis, you know? When's the last time you played Elvis, anyway?

LOU. Five years ago?

(She gives him a look.)

Maybe longer. Do you want me to go?

SANDY. No! I've got a full day of weddings ahead of me. I need you.

LOU. *(music to his ears)* You do?

SANDY. Yes. We'll try it out today. And if it goes all right, maybe I can use you until I find a permanent minister.

(She places the flowers she brought out earlier, straightens the room.)

LOU. What happened to your last one? Was he too old?

SANDY. Too unreliable. That didn't keep me from marrying him, though. Four times, God help me.

LOU. You married him four times? That means you divorced him three.

SANDY. You're good with math.

LOU. So where is he?

SANDY. Look, we've got a celebrity coming in. Two celebrities, actually. Their press agent made it very clear they want everything perfect. These things are always more trouble than they're worth.

LOU. They sure are.

SANDY. Have you done many celebrity weddings?

LOU. Oh yeah. Over the years, dozens. And big stars, too. Paul and Joanne. Steve and Edie. Burt and Angie. Zsa Zsa and – , I forgot, but I married her several times.

SANDY. And recently?

LOU. I don't recall so much. You know, today's stars aren't like the old stars. They're just not as – *big.*

(Enter **VANESSA WELLS** *and* **BRYCE CANNON.**)

VANESSA. Hello, fans, hello. Let us by please. Sorry, no time for autographs. We love you, too. Let us through, let us through.

BRYCE. Watch the coat, watch the coat. Look at all these fans! Yes, we love you, too. Let us through.

(They march into the chapel – two beautiful people in their 50s. Each is impeccably dressed. They take several steps into the room and pose.)

VANESSA. We have arrived.

BRYCE. You may take our things.

(Each simultaneously hands out their coat/hat/purse. They stand frozen until **SANDY** *approaches.)*

SANDY. Oh, okay, um, let me get that. I'll just put them over here, okay?

(She places the items on her desk.)

You must be…

VANESSA. Vanessa Wells!

BRYCE. And Bryce Cannon!

(They strike the pose they always strike when they announce themselves.)

SANDY. Yes, of course. Well, it's certainly an honor to have you with us today. I hope you found the chapel without too much trouble.

VANESSA. We were practically mobbed outside!

BRYCE. They almost tore this jacket right off of me!

LOU. *(at the door)* I don't see anybody out there.

VANESSA. Well, they were there. *Mobs* of them.

BRYCE. *Throngs.*

VANESSA. *Hordes.* And who could blame them? Two of Hollywood's biggest stars getting married? A dream wedding of momentous proportions.

BRYCE. Two luminaries of unspeakable achievement in stage –

VANESSA. Screen –

BRYCE. And philanthropy.

VANESSA. Two of the world's most beautiful people.

BRYCE. If we may say so without conceit.

VANESSA. Now uniting our empires – and our lives – in the holy bonds of matrimony.

BRYCE. What an occasion for the world to celebrate.

(*They join hands and sigh.*)

SANDY. Yes, yes, it most certainly is. Quite the occasion.

(*They beam.*)

LOU. So you two are actors, huh?

(**VANESSA** *and* **BRYCE** *lose their perfect smiles.*)

VANESSA. (*to* **SANDY**) Who is this little man?

SANDY. (*laughing*) This is Lou and he's a real kidder. He knows who you are.

(*aside, sternly to* **LOU**)

Sit down and be quiet!

LOU. Have you been in any pitchers I would know?

BRYCE. We do not make "pitchers."

VANESSA. We make films.

BRYCE. We make art.

VANESSA. We make movies, if you must. But we do not – make –

VANESSA & BRYCE. *Pitchers.*

LOU. Oh. Okay. Have you been in any movies I would know?

(They close their eyes. Must they go through this yet again?)

BRYCE. *(with strained patience)* Well, there was that one little movie I was in – won eight Academy Awards – called *The Cold, Cold River*. I had a minor but pivotal role. Perhaps you heard of that one?

VANESSA. He was brilliant. *Brilliant.*

LOU. I don't think so.

VANESSA. Surely you recall my portrayal of Mother Theresa in the independent film *The Saint of Calcutta*. I gave a performance that many called utterly inspired.

BRYCE. *Ah, yes!*

LOU. It's not ringing a bell.

BRYCE. And of course you were glorious as the head servant in that BBC production of *Mary Queen of Scots*.

VANESSA. As were you in the Budapest remake of *Gone With The Wind* where you played a riveting Hungarian Ashley Wilkes.

BRYCE. Thank you, my pet.

LOU. *(shaking his head)* I'm sorry.

BRYCE. *(a last ditch effort, told reluctantly)* Well, we actually did a television series – together – many years ago, when we were much younger.

*(*VANESSA *sighs unhappily.)*

It was hugely successful. I imagine even *you* would remember it. We played a pair of newlywed spies who did the majority of our espionage while on –

(He finally spits it out.)

Surfboards.

LOU. The Surfin' Secret Agents! Now I remember you! That show was huge! Yeah. Of course. *(beat)* Wow, you've gotten old.

VANESSA. *(controlled)* It was 30 years ago. Of course we've gotten older. But we haven't aged, oh no.

BRYCE. We've matured.

VANESSA. We've blossomed.

BRYCE. We've perfected our bodies and our minds.

VANESSA. Pursued careers of great critical acclaim.

BRYCE. Perfected our crafts, rejecting the common, commercial scripts they offered us, and choosing, instead, films of real substance and matter.

LOU. *(sympathizing)* You couldn't get jobs after the show, huh?

VANESSA. Who is this little man and *must* he be here?

SANDY. *(to LOU through her teeth)* Can you give it a rest?

> *(to VANESSA)*

> Lou is one of the most experienced ministers in all of Las Vegas. He's married all the biggest stars. Only the best for you. Why don't we get started with the wedding? Will anyone else be joining us?

VANESSA. *(looking around and noticing for the first time)* Where are the reporters? There are supposed to be reporters. What is a wedding without reporters!

SANDY. I'm sorry. Was I supposed to arrange for the press?

BRYCE. I thought your agent was handling that.

VANESSA. No, my agent is in the Caribbean finalizing my latest divorce. Your agent was supposed to handle it.

BRYCE. Well, I'm sure he did then.

VANESSA. Call him. *Call him!*

> *(BRYCE pulls out cell phone and dials. Awkward silence as he waits.)*

SANDY. Your outfit is just lovely.

VANESSA. Of course it is.

BRYCE. Monte, it's Bryce. We're down here at the chapel. Where are the reporters? – No, not a one. – Did you tell them 11:00? – Did you tell them the right place? – Well, there's no one here, Monte. No one. And she's *pissed.*

VANESSA. *(grabbing the phone from* **BRYCE***)* Monte, you idiot! How'd you manage to screw this up, huh? We are standing here, both of us looking fabulous for the cameras, and you know what? No cameras. No press. Just some strange little man ogling and harassing me. This is not the grand publicity event we discussed, Monte. You know why? Because a publicity event requires *publicity*! Now you get on the phone and get me some reporters. *People, Us, Entertainment Weekly, The Star, National Enquirer* – I want them all down here to record and celebrate our *blessed union!!*

(She hangs up. Beat.)

LOU. So how long you kids been in love?

(They both turn to him with a look as if to say, are you kidding me?)

VANESSA. I need a drink. What have you got?

SANDY. We have champagne in the back.

VANESSA. Get it.

BRYCE. You sure about that, pet? I mean, you're just out of the tank. You're barely dry.

VANESSA. Get. It. How else am I going to make it through this day?

SANDY. I'll be right back.

(She sends a reproachful look to **LOU** *to behave.)*

LOU. I had an uncle that was a lush. He drowned while taking a shower.

VANESSA. Who chose this chapel? Your agent or mine?

LOU. And when they found him the next day, he was still standing up. Dead, but standing. Can you believe it?

VANESSA. Whichever one it is, he's fired. Call Monte again. See how he's doing.

BRYCE. We just hung up.

VANESSA. You can't tell me the world isn't interested in this event. For God's sake, we're Vanessa Wells!

BRYCE. And Bryce Cannon!

VANESSA. Thirty years ago they would have killed for this story. They would have given anything to see us get together in real life.

SANDY. *(scurrying in with a bottle of champagne and a glass)* I'm back! Did I miss anything?

(VANESSA grabs the bottle and drinks straight from it. SANDY holds the glass awkwardly.)

VANESSA. We were America's sweethearts! With our skimpy wet suits. And our perfect bodies. And our windswept hair that never seemed to get wet even as we surfed 20-foot waves in pursuit of Russian spies and other traitors to the nation. The world couldn't get enough of us.

(VANESSA and BRYCE "surf" during the above.)

BRYCE. Agent 76!

VANESSA. And Agent 44!

BRYCE. We'd find our fans hiding in our dressing room closets.

VANESSA. In the trunks of our cars.

BRYCE. Underneath tables in restaurants.

VANESSA. Behind bushes.

BRYCE. Under piles of leaves!

VANESSA. We were on the cover of every magazine for *years.* All the interviews. The press events. The action figures. I can still hear the crowds calling out to us. Vanessa! Bryce! Can I have an autograph, *please*? That idiot show made us the biggest stars in the *world.*

BRYCE. And the mail we used to get! Do you know they had to hire a whole staff at the studio just to handle our mail?

SANDY. I believe it.

(LOU appears to be looking for something.)

VANESSA. Lose something, little man?

LOU. I was just looking for the restroom.

SANDY. It's in the back.

VANESSA. I thought you worked here.

(**SANDY** *and* **LOU** *exchange a guilty look.*)

I knew it! I knew there no way this little man was a professional minister.

SANDY. No, he is. He really is. My regular minister just wasn't "available" today. So I had to hire Lou, that's all.

VANESSA. Not available? For the biggest wedding this town has seen in decades? Vanessa Wells!

BRYCE. And Bryce Cannon!

SANDY. Well, it's a long story. You're really not interested in my problems.

VANESSA. Au contraire. I would *love* to hear about your problems. I am so tired of thinking about mine. Tell all, please. Go ahead, chapel proprietor, spill.

(*She plops down in a chair.*)

BRYCE. Vanessa! What are you thinking! Wrinkles!

(*She shrieks and touches her face.*)

Not on your face. Your dress. Isn't that linen?

(*She jumps up.*)

VANESSA. Oh my! Thank you, Bryce. A momentary lapse. I'll just take it off until the press arrives.

(*She removes her dress then takes a seat in her slip, still holding the champagne.* **LOU** *looks on appreciatively.*)

BRYCE. You know, I think I'll do the same.

(*He removes his pants and sits.*)

We learned this on the set. Never sit in your costume. Not if you want to look your best, which is, of course, all that matters.

VANESSA. Little man, put your eyes back in your head. I thought you had to go to the bathroom.

LOU. (*still ogling*) I can wait.

VANESSA. (*to* **SANDY**, *indicating dress*) Hang this please, and continue with your story.

BRYCE. *(handing her his pants)* Yes, amuse us, please with your tale of woe.

SANDY. Wow, this isn't getting weird at all, is it?

(She proceeds to hang the clothing.)

Okay, the story of Sandy and Ken. I'll give you the abridged version. Sandy and Ken fall in love. Ken continues falling in love with various other women throughout their marriages. I say marriages because Sandy would get fed up, divorce Ken, change her mind, take him back, and after many promises from Ken, marry him again. And again and again. Did I mention that Ken also drinks too much? This is the part that affects Sandy's business. During one of their longer breaks, Sandy opens a wedding chapel. Ken tracks her down as usual, promises her the moon as usual, and even goes so far as to become an ordained minister to try and wheedle his way back into her life.

LOU. Does it work?

SANDY. Yes, it works. Otherwise, we'd have no story, would we? And now, not only does Ken wreak havoc with Sandy's emotional life, but her professional life as well, since he frequently shows up intoxicated for work, or not all. Which is why you're here. And why I'm such an idiot.

VANESSA. Ah, women! We're all such idiots. Why do we let men manipulate us and ruin our lives?

SANDY. Because we love them?

VANESSA. Because we hate *ourselves.*

SANDY. We do?

VANESSA. We must. Otherwise, why would we stand for such callous behavior? Why would we put up with the rogues and the cads and the scoundrels?

SANDY. Because we're weak?

VANESSA. Because we're strong!

SANDY. I'm not very good at this, am I?

VANESSA. Only a strong woman can endure a man who cheats and drinks and loses her entire fortune at the black jack table – and yet forges ahead to a better life.

SANDY. Oh, Ken's not a gambler.

VANESSA. I'm not talking about *your* life. Do you know how much money I made – we made – doing that idiot show? Do you know how long it took my first husband to lose it all at the Sands?

(She snaps her fingers.)

BRYCE. And yet, you survived!

VANESSA. Yes! I survived and went on to marry the Baron, a wonderful man who, unfortunately, enjoyed wearing ladies lingerie. And then there was the Senator who only wanted me for my fame and connections. And the record producer who only married me for my money. Was he surprised! Ha!

BRYCE. And finally…for some inconceivable reason, there was the plumber.

VANESSA. Yes, the plumber, who at this very moment is in a Caribbean courtroom trying to take the last of the little money I have left.

BRYCE. What were you *thinking?*

VANESSA. I don't know, Bryce. I don't know.

BRYCE. And yet, you survived!

VANESSA. Yes, I survived. As did you!

BRYCE. It's true. I made a few bad decisions over the years, made some bad investments, trusted the wrong people –

VANESSA. His own brother.

BRYCE. And found myself, like Vanessa, deprived of all of my Secret Agent earnings. At one point, I will admit to you and you only, I was living in a trailer, ashamed to show my face to the other trailer park residents for fear of being recognized and pitied.

VANESSA. I didn't realize it had gotten *that* bad.

BRYCE. Oh yes.

VANESSA. You should have called me, pet.

BRYCE. I did. You were in the tank.

VANESSA. Oh, sorry. *(beat)* Which time?

BRYCE. Hard to say.

LOU. Well, that's just a cryin' shame, that is. Both of you losing everything you worked for!

VANESSA. But we went on, little man, we went on!

BRYCE. We used our talent –

VANESSA. And our beauty!

BRYCE. – to claw our way back.

VANESSA. But beauty is such a double edged sword. You can both count yourselves lucky that you haven't been cursed with it. Bryce, tell them how difficult it is to be beautiful.

BRYCE. Ah, the assumptions that you must be dim. The lecherous advances from those with power. The expectations of fans that you will never age. And the disappointment when they see that, alas, you have.

VANESSA. How could we possibly look as good today as we did 30 years ago? It's physically impossible.

BRYCE. And yet, somehow, I do.

VANESSA. Come again?

BRYCE. Well, look at me. I'm flawless. Not an extra pound anywhere. Perhaps a few crow's feet, but barely noticeable. Some grey around the temples, but that's considered sexy in men. All in all, I'm fabulous.

VANESSA. And I'm not?

BRYCE. Well, yes, but just not as fabulous as me. I mean it's different for women. Things – fall.

(**VANESSA** *gasps.*)

VANESSA. How dare you?

BRYCE. It's just the inescapable truth, Van. In the aging department, men fare much better. Sorry 'bout that.

(*to* **LOU**)

Right, buddy?

LOU. I don't know if it's true or not, but this is no way to talk to the woman you love.

VANESSA. Love? Ha! The only person he loves or has ever loved is himself!

BRYCE. Says the woman with a 5-foot picture of herself in her livingroom.

VANESSA. Says the man who tattooed his own name on his *chest*!

*(***BRYCE** *gasps.)*

BRYCE. I told you that in confidence!

VANESSA. Don't take me on, Bryce. I know waaaaay too much. San Francisco. 1982!

BRYCE. And I don't know things? Monte Carlo. 1999.

(They eye each other carefully and appear to reach a stalemate.)

Yes, well, we both have our pasts.

VANESSA. But we don't care about the past any more. It's the future we're looking towards, right?

BRYCE. Right.

VANESSA. We just need to get our names out there again.

BRYCE. Remind America of how much they loved us!

VANESSA. Bring back the old magic! We can do it, Bryce, I know we can! Where are the reporters!? Call that agent of yours right now. Find out what's happening.

*(***BRYCE** *dials.)*

BRYCE. Monte. What's happening? Uh huh. Uh huh. Did you call – ? Uh huh. What about – ? Okay. So that's where we stand? Okay. Thanks.

(He hangs up.)

VANESSA. Well?

BRYCE. No one's coming.

VANESSA. No one's coming?

BRYCE. No. They have no interest in this story.

VANESSA. But why? Why aren't they interested?

BRYCE. I don't know!

VANESSA. Well, call him back! I want to know *why* they're not interested. This makes no sense. We've got a bonafide news story here, and I won't be satisfied until I know why! Call, call!

BRYCE. All right!

(He dials.)

Monte, it's me again. Vanessa wants to know why –

VANESSA. *(grabbing the phone from him)* Why aren't they interested, Monte? You said they would be. You said this would catapult us back into the news. You said this was our big comeback! How could they not be – What? – I see. – Uh huh, and that's the reason. Okay. I see.

*(She hangs up and hands the phone to **BRYCE**.)*

BRYCE. Well?

VANESSA. You're right. They're not interested.

BRYCE. Did he tell you why?

VANESSA. Yes, he did. *(beat)* It seems everyone already knows... *(pause)* ...that you're gay. You haven't hidden it as well as you thought. And if you're gay, why would we be getting married unless it was just a publicity stunt? And if it's just a publicity stunt, they're not interested. Especially one involving a couple of washed up old celebrities. And I quote.

BRYCE. We are not old! *(beat)* Everybody knows I'm gay?

SANDY. I kinda suspected. Just because you're so pretty.

LOU. Well, I had no idea! You're so tall.

VANESSA. Well, I guess that's that.

(She retrieves her dress and begins dressing.)

BRYCE. Everyone knows, huh?

VANESSA. Apparently so.

BRYCE. Well, it's a relief actually. Good. I'm glad. I'm mean, it's not like it's going to hurt my career or anything, right?

(He laughs. He gets his pants.)

VANESSA. *(laughing)* Not really. Your career couldn't get much worse!

BRYCE. *(not laughing)* Nor could yours, my pet, nor could yours!

VANESSA. Well, I have done numerous independent films in the last few years –

BRYCE. Student films! Let's be honest – it's just us.

VANESSA. All right, student films! At least mine have been in *English.*

BRYCE. At least I've been playing pivotal roles, not maids and servants.

VANESSA. Pivotal roles? Do you know who he played in his Academy Award winning film? The corpse on the examining table!

BRYCE. All right, all right! Why are we attacking each other? It's that damn show that did it all.

VANESSA. That idiot show!

BRYCE. *(to* **SANDY** *and* **LOU***)* Do you know what happens when you play a surfing secret agent for five years? No one takes you seriously anymore.

VANESSA. No one hires you because you've become a joke!

BRYCE. A fool!

VANESSA. A clown! The reporters are right. We're washed up. Yesterday's news. Complete and total –

VANESSA & BRYCE. Has beens.

(They are deflated.)

LOU. Oh, come on, kids. It's not that bad. We've all had our low moments. But we come back, we survive. You said so yourself. Well, look at me. My precious wife of 40 years died a year ago. And I couldn't have been any lower. But finally, I got myself out of the house, I said, I'm going back to work. But who would give an old guy like me a chance? This nice little lady here. So even when you think you're washed up, opportunity knocks.

SANDY. That's right. You never know what's waiting for you right around the corner.

VANESSA. They don't understand.

BRYCE. No. How could they?

VANESSA. Chapel proprietor, little man, we appreciate the story, but we're talking about fame here. Fame of the highest order. We had it once and we will have it again!

BRYCE. Yes, we will!

VANESSA. The only question is, how are we going to get it? We need a new plan. A new plot.

BRYCE. What if –

VANESSA. Yes?

BRYCE. What if we announce that one of us is dying?

VANESSA. *(intrigued)* Yes, yes?

BRYCE. Of something tragic, incurable. I can see the headlines in the *Star* now, Vanessa Wells Stricken. Faithful Friend at Her Bedside.

VANESSA. Why do I have to be the one that's dying?

BRYCE. *(arms outstretched)* Look at me.

VANESSA. All right, all right! What happens when months pass and I don't die?

BRYCE. You got better.

VANESSA. I thought it was incurable.

BRYCE. They were wrong. And then we have another story. Vanessa Wells Miracle Recovery. Faithful Friend at Her Side.

VANESSA. And you're the faithful friend?

BRYCE. Of course.

VANESSA. I don't know. Maybe. How about this – what if we announce that you're gay?

BRYCE. I thought everybody already knew?

VANESSA. Yes, but we *officially* announce it. And you give your firsthand account of the pain and shame of hiding your secret. Bryce Cannon Gay Admission. Faithful Friend at His Side.

BRYCE. I don't think it's enough of story. Not today anyway.

(Idea!)

What if we announce that you're gay, too? Both of the Surfin' Secret Agents – gay and gayer! Now *there's* a story.

VANESSA. Now who's going to believe that I'm a lesbian?

SANDY. Well, you were very athletic on the show. I mean, you could really handle those waves.

VANESSA. Those were stunt doubles, for God's sake.

LOU. Vanessa Wells gay. Wow. I'm speechless. And she's been married all those times.

VANESSA. I am not gay, you ridiculous little man.

LOU. You don't have to be ashamed about it. Be proud of who you are. I'm just very surprised. I guess the wedding's really off now.

BRYCE. See? We'd have no trouble selling the story.

VANESSA. No, I won't do it. I won't be gay! We'll just have to think of something else.

BRYCE. Well, there's always the other thing.

VANESSA. Oh, God, not that.

BRYCE. Maybe we've gotten to the point where we have to consider it.

SANDY. Consider what?

BRYCE. The Surfin' Secret Agents Reunion Special: 30 Years Later.

VANESSA. Nothing says you're washed up like a reunion special!

BRYCE. But there's interest in the project. They've been calling our agents.

VANESSA. It means going back! Back to that idiotic show that ruined our lives!

BRYCE. Yes, but it would get us on TV. In front of the cameras once again. Imagine it, Miss Wells, would you take your place on the set, please? Miss Wells, come to makeup please. Miss Wells, it's time for your costume fitting. Miss Wells, would you sign some autographs, please?

VANESSA. Yes, well, that does all sound very nice –

BRYCE. Who knows what producers may be watching. They'll see how fabulous we still look. And how wonderfully we still work together.

VANESSA. Yes, yes.

BRYCE. It could be the beginning of big things for us! Let's do it, Van!

VANESSA. *(succumbing)* All right, all right. Call Monte, tell him we're in. Tell him to call the press!

BRYCE. This time tomorrow, we could be back!

VANESSA. Oh my goodness, there's so much to be done! We must be on our way! Little man, go outside and clear away the fans so that we can pass.

LOU. Huh?

SANDY. You heard her. Go clear away the fans.

LOU. But there's nobody –

SANDY. Go.

(*LOU goes outside.*)

LOU. *(outside)* Clear the way! Clear the way! The stars are coming out!

SANDY. Miss Wells, Mr. Cannon, I'm sorry today didn't work out, but I wish you the best for the future.

VANESSA. And what a future it will be! You'll be hearing all about us very soon! Bryce, prepare yourself for the throngs!

BRYCE. Look out world, we're coming back!

VANESSA. Vanessa Wells!

BRYCE. And Bryce Cannon!

VANESSA. *(as they exit)* No pushing please. Let us through!

BRYCE. Watch the coat! Watch the coat!

(*After a moment,* **LOU** *reenters.*)

LOU. I'm telling you, there was nobody out there. What a pair, huh?

SANDY. Yeah. *(pause)* Look, Lou, I don't think this is going to work out.

LOU. Really?

SANDY. You're a nice man, but I don't know if this is the right business for you – any more.

LOU. But I need to do *something* or I'll go crazy. I've gotta get out of the house.

SANDY. You ever think of volunteering your time?

LOU. Doing what?

SANDY. How about a retirement home. You could perform for the residents – as Elvis!

LOU. Hmm.

SANDY. And they're a captive crowd.

LOU. It would be nice to do the old act again. And you know, when I've got my costume and my sideburns on, you can barely tell us apart, me and Elvis.

SANDY. Is that right?

LOU. Yeah. Maybe sometime when I'm performing, you'll come and see my show. And I'll take you out for dinner afterwards.

SANDY. Are you asking me out?

LOU. Well, not right now, but the next time you divorce your husband, give me a call.

SANDY. Okay, Lou. I'll be sure to do that.

LOU. It was nice meeting you, Sandy.

SANDY. Nice meeting you, too. Good luck out there.

(They shake hands. **LOU** *exits.)*

Crazy little man.

(Curtain closes.)

Marvin & Fiona: The Real Thing

(Months later. **SANDY** *is seated at the desk, reading a romance novel. Enter* **MARVIN**. *He wears a rumpled suit and bow tie. He is a mild-mannered guy. He stands, holding a small parcel, waiting for her to notice him. He clears his throat. He takes a step towards her. He continues to wait. He clears his throat again.)*

SANDY. *(sing-song)* Just a moment.

MARVIN. Sorry.

SANDY. I'm just getting to the good part.

MARVIN. Well, that's quite all right, ma'am. I'll just wait here until you're done.

(She reads for what feels like a long time. He waits.)

SANDY. Mmm, mmm, mmm!

(She closes the book.)

Ever read a Harlequin romance?

MARVIN. I don't believe I have, ma'am. But I've got all the romance I need.

SANDY. Is that right? What have you got there?

MARVIN. Oh. This was outside your door. I couldn't help but notice that there are no directions from the sender authorizing that it could be left in an unprotected space. And unless *you* filed a written order to that effect, your mail carrier has committed a gross violation of the Postal Code.

SANDY. Oh my.

MARVIN. Yes. It's best not to let this kind of conduct go. I would recommend that you speak to your mail carrier about the matter. And if you are not satisfied, talk to your local postmaster.

SANDY. *(taking the package from him)* Well, aren't you – official? Thank you. Was there anything else?

MARVIN. Well, yes. I'm Marvin Marvel. I'm getting married today. I should be on your schedule for five o'clock.

SANDY. Marvin Marvel?

MARVIN. Yes.

SANDY. Dear God. The kids must have had fun with you.

MARVIN. Yes ma'am.

SANDY. *(looking at computer screen)* Marvin Marvel. Marvvvv-in Marvel. I'm not seeing you.

MARVIN. I'm sure it's there. Look again please.

SANDY. I see a reservation for a *Martin* Marvel.

MARVIN. Well, that's me, of course. I'm sure it was just a typographical error. Martin, Marvin. It happens all the time.

SANDY. People call you Martin all the time?

MARVIN. No, typographical errors. They happen all the time. That's one of the leading reasons mail doesn't get properly delivered to its intended destination despite the best efforts of the U.S. Postal Service. You should see some of the misspelled envelopes we get. Some of the best laughs I've ever had! Let me tell you. By golly.

(He smiles, sighs.)

SANDY. Marvin, is there a bride somewhere?

MARVIN. Yes, ma'am. She's just fixing her make-up in the car.

SANDY. Oh good. So, just guessing here, and I've gotten pretty good at this over the years, I'd say you're from – Salt Lake City. But not necessarily Mormon. Your bride is an elementary school teacher. And you've been sweethearts all your lives. Now, why are you getting married in Vegas? *That* is always the toughest part. Seems to me you'd be getting married in your church surrounded by family and friends and the local postal squad.

MARVIN. My family and friends don't approve of the wedding.

SANDY. Don't help me. I can do this.

MARVIN. And they don't approve of Fiona.

SANDY. Fiona! How could they not approve of Fiona? Sweet, innocent, Midwestern, child-loving Fiona?

(Enter **FIONA**, *dressed in leather and sporting tattoos. She and* **MARVIN** *couldn't possibly be more different. She backs in, yelling out the door.)*

FIONA. Oh yeah, dickwad? Well, you come on inside and say that, you piece of Peeping Tom shit! My fiancé will jack you up like you ain't ever been jacked, you punkass mother... *(pause)* "f"-errrrrr!

SANDY. Okay, I was a little off.

MARVIN. Is someone bothering you, angel?

FIONA. *(still yelling out the door)* Just some *punkass* watchin' me change my clothes in the car. Yeah, you better run, *you yellow freakin' lizard shit!!*

(Beat. To **MARVIN**, *sweet)*

Hey, baby. We all set to get married?

MARVIN. Yeah, I think so. You like the place?

FIONA. *(looking around)* Oh Marvin. It's like a dream. I never thought I'd be gettin' married in a place so classy. With a beautiful altar. And real flowers. And, oh my god, real pews! I wish Fist could see this. *He* wanted to marry me in a toilet stall. I'm so lucky I found you, Marvin.

MARVIN. We're lucky we found each other.

(He takes her hand.)

How come you took off the wedding dress, angel? You looked so nice in it.

FIONA. It just wasn't me, baby. The lace was itchin' me, and all that white was a nightmare, like I'd been sentenced to church for 100 years or somethin', you know?

MARVIN. Yeah.

FIONA. I'm tryin' to change for you, baby, I really am. Hey, did you notice before I said mother "f"-er. I stopped myself from sayin' the whole word.

MARVIN. I sure did. And I'm proud of you.

FIONA. It's just that I can't change too much at a time, or else I'm afraid my atoms might get too confused. And when your atoms get confused, there's no telling what might happen. I read all about it in *Ladies Home Journal*. People with confused atoms sometimes turn into hermaphrodites. *(pronounced "her-ma-phro-dit-ties".)* You know what that is? It's like a half-man, half-woman thing.

MARVIN. Oh, angel, I don't think that could happen.

FIONA. Well, just in case, I'm gonna take it slow, okay?

MARVIN. Okay.

FIONA. I mean, you still like me like this, right?

MARVIN. I love you like this.

(They join hands. Big sigh.)

SANDY. Okay, I just have to say this. You two are *fascinating*. And I haven't been fascinated by anything that happened here in a long time. We're talking 17 years of weddings that have included circus freaks, celebrities, psychopaths, even a pair of conjoined twins marrying another pair of conjoined twins. None of them captured my attention the way you two have. Bravo.

(She applauds.)

FIONA. What's with this bitch? Is she disrespectin' us?

SANDY. No. No disrespect.

FIONA. *(approaching her)* Callin' us circus freaks? I'll freak *you* up.

SANDY. No, you misunderstand.

FIONA. I'll take you out back and show you a little somethin' I learned in the big house. Give you a little state-issued overhaul, if you know what I'm sayin'.

SANDY. *AND* you're an ex-con? You have so made my day. Thank you. Thank you for choosing my wedding chapel. You don't know how boring it can get here day after day. Now I want details. I want to hear everything about you. Come, have a seat. Let's chat. Please.

(They hesitate then sit, **FIONA** *warily.)*

SANDY. *(cont.)* There you go. That's it. So, how did you two kids meet? And don't leave out a thing. Tell Aunt Sandy *everything.*

MARVIN. Well, okay. But you are going to marry us, right?

SANDY. Of course, of course. Let's just get to know each other a little first. I don't have another wedding scheduled for forty-five minutes.

MARVIN. All right. Well, we met online. Three years, two months and 17 days ago.

FIONA. Ain't it somethin' how he counts the days?

MARVIN. I was lonely. My whole life, women were never interested in me. Or anything I was interested in. I didn't know how to talk to them in person. So I started chatting online and one night I met Fiona.

FIONA. *(snapping her fingers)* ZipItBitchFromCellBlock2!

MARVIN. And I was MarvelousMarvin.

FIONA. Not at first, remember? At first he was just MarvinMarvel. And I said to him, dude, you're not supposed to use your real name.

MARVIN. And she suggested I be MarvelousMarvin.

FIONA. Because he was. Is! So marvelous.

SANDY. So, Marvin, what exactly was it that first attracted you to, uh, ZipItBitch?

MARVIN. Now that's a funny story, ma'am. I thought she might be someone with a similar affection for the postal code. I thought we might talk about the 9-digit zip code and the effects it's had on mail delivery.

FIONA. Yeah, he didn't know that was my slammer name! I was always tellin' anyone who got in my face to "Zip it, bitch!" So the name just stuck.

SANDY. How about that. So even after you learned she was an inmate –

FIONA. *(annoyed, correcting her)* Convict.

SANDY. Excuse me?

FIONA. I was a convict, not an inmate.

MARVIN. You see, ma'am, in prison vernacular, there's a big difference. Inmate is a derogatory term. Only guards or new arrivals who don't know the lingo yet say inmate. Everyone else says convict. It shows respect, see?

FIONA. *(beaming with pride)* You have learned so much. He could go into any prison anywhere in the country and speak the language beautifully.

MARVIN. *(blushing)* Well, you're a good teacher.

FIONA. No, you're a good teacher. What I have learned from this man – about enjoyin' the little things in life, and seein' the good in others, and forgivin' yourself for not being perfect. I didn't like myself very much before I met Marvin. But somehow he saw things in me to like that nobody else ever saw.

SANDY. I can't imagine what. I mean, how about that?

MARVIN. Yes, once you get past all the fighting and the cursing and the criminal record and the powerful right cross, she's a very sweet girl.

(They gaze lovingly at each other.)

SANDY. Can I ask you – what were you in for?

FIONA. Bank job. Yeah, I know.

(She gets up.)

Fist talked me into drivin' the getaway car. It was my own fault for goin' along. Naturally, his plan was stupid, and we got caught and I wound up with 15 to 25. Fist got even more 'cause he was the mastermind. Mastermind! Ain't that a joke. Thank God he's out of my life forever.

(beat)

Anyway, at first, talkin' to Marvin just helped me pass the time. But I figured out pretty quick there was somethin' special about this guy. He knew so much stuff! And when it comes to postal regulations, forget about it.

MARVIN. Oh, stop, angel.

FIONA. No, seriously, he knows everything there is to know. Like thousands of pages worth of stuff. You can ask him anything. Like – what size does a mail slot have to be?

MARVIN. The clear rectangular opening in the outside slot plate must be at least 1 ½ inches wide and 7 inches long, and the bottom of the slot must be at least 30 inches above the finished floor line.

(He shrugs.)

SANDY. Huh.

FIONA. What's the biggest thing you can mail?

MARVIN. Generally speaking, no mailpiece may weigh more than 70 pounds, and except for Parcel Post, no mailpiece may measure more than 108 inches in length and girth combined.

FIONA. Can you mail…an animal?

MARVIN. Some animals, yes, if they don't require food or water or attention during handling in the mail, and if they don't create sanitary problems or obnoxious odors.

SANDY. Really? Like what?

MARVIN. Certain types of fowl and your basic small cold-blooded animals.

FIONA. Like baby alligators?

MARVIN. *(pleased)* Yes, you remembered. And earthworms, salamanders, lizards, snails.

FIONA. Snakes?

MARVIN. No snakes.

FIONA. What about a turkey?

MARVIN. You can mail turkeys, doves, ducks, geese, swans…

SANDY. What about a cat or a dog?

MARVIN. No, you can't mail any warm-blooded animals, except for a few specified birds.

FIONA. How about bees?

MARVIN. Yes.

SANDY. Insects?

MARVIN. Yep.

FIONA. Live scorpions?

MARVIN. Sure can. But you must secure them in a double mailing container. We don't want them breaking free!

(He runs his fingers up her arm like a scorpion.)

FIONA. *(laughing)* See what I mean? You can't stump him! And I've been tryin' for three years!

MARVIN. And two months and 17 days!

SANDY. You two are surprisingly – sweet. I'm guessing, since you're sitting here, you must have been paroled early.

FIONA. Yeah, I was. Again, thanks to Marvin. My first couple a years in the joint, I was always in trouble, always fightin' in the yard. But Marvin, he showed me that the smart thing to do was to keep my mouth shut and play by the rules. So that's what I did. I did my shifts in the kitchen without complaining, kept to myself, and got paroled after 6 ½ years for good behavior. Yesterday.

SANDY. Yesterday?

MARVIN. Yes, ma'am! I picked her up at the Tucson Federal Correctional Institute in the afternoon and we drove straight to Las Vegas last night. And here we are.

SANDY. Oh my goodness. Is this the first time you two have actually met?

MARVIN. Oh no. I've visited her in jail many times over the years.

FIONA. This sweet man would drive all the way from Wilber, Nebraska to see me for two hours, and then turn around and go all the way home.

SANDY. To Tucson? That's got to be a thousand miles.

MARVIN. Closer to twelve hundred.

FIONA. You shoulda seen the day he proposed to me. He comes into the visitor's room wearin' a tuxedo, kneels down on one knee, and right there in front of everybody says, Fiona, would you make me the happiest man in the world and marry me? I was cryin' so much I could hardly talk. Even Fatass, that was the head guard, we called her Fatass for obvious reasons, even she was cryin'. And we decided right then and there, the day I got paroled, we'd drive straight to Las Vegas and get married. Everyone in the cell block got in on it. They helped me pick out the wedding chapel and make all the arrangements. It gave us all something happy to think about, you know.

SANDY. That's beautiful.

(to **MARVIN**)

You're quite the romantic, aren't you?

MARVIN. According to my mother, I'm quite the lunatic.

FIONA. Your brother, too.

MARVIN. Yes. I wish they were here to help us celebrate. But they don't understand. I told them, you have to look past the exterior and see what's inside. That's why Fiona and I are so happy. We were able to do that. But they can't. When I showed my mother a picture of Fiona she called her a – I can't say it.

FIONA. She called me a slut. And when I showed my mother a picture of Marvin, she called him a fruit.

MARVIN. She did?

FIONA. Sorry, baby. It's just that you're so different from any guy I ever went out with. In a good way!

(to **SANDY**)

See, I always went for the losers that were gonna get me in trouble and ruin my life. It was like a fatal flaw, ya know?

SANDY. I hear you, sister. I've married the same guy four times. I just divorced him again last month and already he's working his way back into my life! Biggest loser you ever want to meet. Drinks too much. Works too little. In fact, he's supposed to be doing your ceremony, but he's passed out in the back room.

MARVIN. What?

SANDY. But what can I say? He's got the bluest eyes you've ever seen.

FIONA. Exactly! All of my men have been the same. Big, tough, handsome men – without a brain in their heads. But hot! The muscles, the tats, the piercings. Fist could lift me over his head with one hand. He was an animal. They all were. Thank god I'm over that!

(**MARVIN** *looks upset.*)

MARVIN. *You know, angel...* I could lift you over my head if you wanted. I just didn't know you wanted that.

FIONA. What?

MARVIN. When I was delivering the mail, I held the record for completing the 10-mile Riverfront Route in just 3 hours and 34 minutes while carrying a *50 pound satchel*, thank you very much. And I'd be more than willing to take on any of your *hot* ex-boyfriends, even Fist if you wanted, and show them a thing or two.

FIONA. Huh?

MARVIN. I've got moves, Fiona. You've just never seen me in action.

(*He demonstrates a move.*)

FIONA. Marvin, what is going on with you? Are you jealous of *Fist?*

MARVIN. You know what I would do if he was here right now?

(**FIST** *enters from the back room. He comes up from behind them. He's a scary-looking guy.*)

MARVIN. *(cont.)* First thing, I'd get him in a headlock. Oh yeah, I know how to do that. I was on the wrestling team. Okay, I never actually wrestled, I was the stop watch guy, but I learned all the moves. So I'd get him in a headlock and I'd spin him around and around and I'd take him down so fast he wouldn't know what hit him. Then I'd squeeze him in the vise that is my arm until he apologized for all the lousy things he did to you...or until he cried for his mommy. *That's* what I'd do.

FIST. *(quietly)* Mama.

MARVIN, FIONA, SANDY. *(after turning and seeing him)* Aaaaaaaaaaaah!

(**MARVIN** *and* **FIONA** *jump.* **SANDY** *scurries under/behind the table.*)

FIST. *(smiling)* Hi, kids. Happy to see me?

FIONA. *(the first to recover)* Fist! What the ffffffffff-frig are you doin' here?

FIST. I was in the neighborhood. Thought I'd drop by.

FIONA. But you're still in jail!

FIST. Oh yeah?

FIONA. You get paroled?

FIST. In a manner of speakin'. I paroled myself.

FIONA. You escaped?!

FIST. Well, I couldn't go missin' the weddin' now, could I?

FIONA. How'd you know about – ?

FIST. There ain't no secrets in the joint, Fiona. You should know that. I got boys in Tuscon and they told me all about it. Said my girl was gittin' married. To some other dude. They even knew which chapel. Naturally, I was none too happy.

FIONA. I ain't your girl! I'd have to be a friggin' idiot to be *your* girl!

FIST. I guess you're still mad, huh? About the bank thing?

FIONA. The bank *thing*? I got 15 years, Fist! And you got 25!

FIST. All right, already. So I made a mistake. At least you got out early.

FIONA. No thanks to you!

FIST. Me? What could I do? I been sitting in jail with Hubcap. He says hi, by the way.

FIONA. That moron. An even worse bank robber than you.

FIST. I'm sensin' a lotta hostility here.

FIONA. What'd you expect? Did ya think I'd be glad to see ya?

FIST. *(innocently, almost hurt)* Well, yeah. I'm your guy.

FIONA. You ain't my guy. He's my guy. And I want you to take your sorry ass out of here and leave us the fffffffff-frig alone!

FIST. After I come all this way? You are cold, Fiona. Cold, cold, cold. *(beat)* And what's with the frig? You used to have a real mouth on ya.

FIONA. I'm tryin' to improve myself. Somethin' you wouldn't know nothin' about.

FIST. Yeah, you're right about that.

> *(beat)*

> It's been a long time. *(not unkindly, just factually)* You look older.

FIONA. Yeah, well you look stupider.

FIST. You grew your hair.

FIONA. You lost some of yours.

FIST. We ain't seen each other in six years, Fiona. Aint you got nothin' nice to say to me?

FIONA. *You ruined my life!*

FIST. *(innocently to* **SANDY**, *who is poking her head over the table)* I'll tell ya, ya do one wrong thing –

> *(He shakes his head. She sympathizes. His attention now falls upon* **MARVIN**.*)*

> So this is the guy, huh? Kinda puny, ain't he?

> *(extending his hand)*

> Fist.

MARVIN. Marvin.

(Very reluctantly **MARVIN** *shakes his hand.* **FIST** *doesn't let go. He squeezes* **MARVIN***'s hand hard driving* **MARVIN** *down on his knees in pain.)*

Aaahhhhhhhhhhhhhhhhhhhhhhh!

FIONA. Let go. Fist, stop it! Let go of him!!!

(She beats on his back. **FIST** *lets go, vindicated.* **MARVIN** *falls to the floor, moaning.* **FIONA** *tends to him.)*

FIST. Nice to meet ya.

FIONA. Baby, are you all right?

(to **FIST***)*

You are an *animal*!

*(***FIST** *looks pleased. During all of this* **SANDY** *has come out from under the desk and is crawling to the back room.)*

FIST. Hey, you! Chapel lady! Get back here. Sit down. I don't need you calling the cops on me.

SANDY. I was just –

FIST. Sit!

SANDY. Yes, Mr. Fist.

(She sits behind the desk.)

FIST. So, I take it the weddin' hasn't happened yet?

SANDY. No Mr. Fist.

FIST. Good. I woulda hated to miss the festivities.

FIONA. What do you want? Why are you here?

FIST. Now that hurts my feelings. You don't want your oldest friend at your wedding?

(to **MARVIN***)*

Fiona and me go way back. We gotta *lotta* history. She ever tell you about us?

MARVIN. *(still recovering on the floor)* Of course.

FIST. She ever tell you about the time we was kids, like 10 or somethin', we stole her old man's car and drove to Atlantic City? The cops stopped us doin' 90 down the Atlantic City Expressway and threw us in jail until her old man came for us. 'Course he was hammered as always and didn't come for two days.

FIONA. How come I always wound up in jail when I was with you?

FIST. Hey, we had some good times. Remember the time we broke into the penthouse of the Waldorf Astoria and stayed for three nights, eatin' and drinkin' everythin' in the mini fridge and doin' it all night long? Fiona can be *insatiable*. I hope you're up for it.

FIONA. You're a pig.

FIST. And you love it, baby! I see you still have my name on your arm.

FIONA. It's coming off as soon as we get home and I find a doctor.

FIST. And where's home? Huh?

MARVIN. *(finally standing up slowly)* I, uh, live in Nebraska.

FIST. *Nebraska!* Holy shit, Fiona. What the "frig" are you gonna do in Nebraska? I don't even know if they have like, roads, in Nebraska.

FIONA. We're gonna make a life.

MARVIN. *(taking her hand)* We're going to make a good life.

FIST. Doin' *what*?

MARVIN. Just ordinary things. Going to work every day. Having dinner at night. Working on our home and our garden. Fiona discovered horticulture in prison and really loves it, so hopefully she'll be able to find a job in that field.

FIST. Horticulture? He's gonna send you out on the streets? Even I wouldn't have done that.

FIONA. Not that kind of whore, you idiot. It's plants and flowers and shit. I mean stuff.

(to **MARVIN***)*

Sorry, baby.

FIST. You hear how she talks to me? This is how she'll be talking to you, my friend. Dude, do you really think Fiona's gonna be happy in Nebraska plantin' flowers? You don't know this girl like I do.

MARVIN. I know her.

FIST. Yeah? What's her favorite color?

MARVIN. Red.

FIST. Wrong. Black. Aint that right, baby?

FIONA. I used to like black. Now I like colors, red most of all.

MARVIN. What's her favorite magazine?

FIST. Magazine? Hell, she don't read!

MARVIN. *Ladies Home Journal.* She read every page of every issue in prison. Where does she dream of going most in the world?

FIST. I know this! Disney World.

FIONA. Yeah. When I was *nine!*

MARVIN. Paris, France. Which is where we're going on our honeymoon. How many kids does she want to have?

FIST. All right, now this I know! After the growing up we had, Fiona don't want no kids.

MARVIN. Three. A boy and a girl and a surprise.

   (beat)

FIST. All right, all right already! I ain't seen Fiona for over six years, so naturally, some things have changed. But here's one thing that don't change, postal boy: where you come from. Fiona and me, we come from nothin' and nowhere. Her daddy used to beat the shit out of her and her mama 'cept on the occasions I come by and stopped him. My mama walked the streets. We come from the same stinkin' place and we got ties that aint ever gonna be broken. Aint that right, Fiona?

FIONA. *(exasperated)* Fist, what do you want from me? Why are you here?

FIST. 'Cause I can't let you marry this corn cob from Nebraska. You're marrying me. Yo! Chapel lady!

SANDY. Yes, Mr. Fist?

FIST. Let's get this wedding going, huh? I got a lotta heat on me, so let's do it!

SANDY. I'll go get the flowers. And the reverend. Hopefully.

(She exits.)

FIST. Well, make it quick.

FIONA. Are you outa your loser mind? I ain't marryin' you.

FIST. Yeah, ya are. You just got all confused in prison. You didn't have no men around ya, and ya met this guy and he was better than nothin' I guess, but daddy's back! So you don't have to go slummin' no more.

FIONA. I ain't slummin'!

FIST. Do you even know this guy?

FIONA. 'Course I do.

FIST. 'Cause I found out some stuff.

FIONA. Oh yeah? How?

FIST. On the computer. The internet.

FIONA. And how'd you do that seein's how you can't read?

FIST. I got my boys to do it for me. Whatever. Don't bust my balls. The thing is, Fiona, this guy's got a past.

FIONA. *(laughing)* Oh yeah?

FIST. Did you know he was an Eagle Scout?

FIONA. Yeah.

FIST. Did you know he teaches Sunday School?

FIONA. Yeah.

FIST. Did you know he volunteers at the *library*?

FIONA. Yeah. So what's your point?

FIST. This guy's gonna bore the shit out of you! Fiona, he writes a column on why zip codes is important.

FIONA. I never fully appreciated that before Marvin explained it to me.

FIST. He's a church-goin', rule-followin' do-gooder from Just Kill Me Already, Nebraska. What kind of life are you gonna have, huh? Fiona, you like excitement, danger, living on the edge. Just like me! But Zippy here, he's gonna put you a coma.

MARVIN. Okay, I must object.

FIST. Who the hell's he objectin' to? We aint in court.

MARVIN. I am not the insufferable bore you're making me out to be. I've done some very exciting things in my life. And I've seen danger.

FIST. This I can't wait to hear. Lay it on me, mailbag.

MARVIN. You ever face down a 200 pound Doberman who's slipped his leash and is planning to have you for lunch?

FIST. *(seems to be embarrassed)* Uh, yeah, as a matter a fact, I have.

MARVIN. What'd you do?

FIST. *(defensively)* Nothin'. The thing attacked me. Wasn't nothin' I could do. Wasn't nothin' nobody could do. He weighed 300 pounds.

FIONA. That dog gets bigger every time you tell it.

(to MARVIN)

Seems nobody on our "advance" team figured out that the bank had a dog. I mean, if you was gonna rob a bank, Marvin, don't you think you'd a known that before going in?

MARVIN. Yes, I believe I would have. I like to do my homework.

FIST. All right, all right! So I made a mistake! Kill me already. What'd you do with *your* dog, big shot?

MARVIN. Well, as you know, the motto of the Scouts is Be Prepared.

FIONA. He don't know that.

(FIST gives her a dirty look.)

MARVIN. So back when I used to deliver the mail, I made sure I was prepared for anything, especially dogs. One time, I go into the Ramsey's yard, I see Damian there, eyeing me up as usual, but this time there's something different. He's a lot closer to me than usual. And then I realize, he's not on the chain. And he's looking me over real good. He's looking at me and seeing a tasty mailman sandwich.

FIONA. Oh, Marvin, you're so funny.

FIST. What's funny about that? That ain't even a joke. I'll tell you a joke: three hookers walk into a bar…

FIONA. Shut up. So what happened with the big dog?

MARVIN. Well, he can see the gate is closed behind me, and there's no way I'm making it over the fence.

FIONA. So what'd you do, baby?

MARVIN. I quickly assess the situation and realize it doesn't look good. But I'm not worried because I've prepared for just this moment.

FIONA. That's my Marvin.

MARVIN. So just before he lunges at me, I reach into my shirt, pull out my emergency postal whistle and blow!

(He pulls a whistle out from his shirt and blows.)

I blow that thing with every breath in my body as birds scatter, cars veer off the road and ol' Damian sees stars. He runs whimpering under the porch, until all I can see are his big white, frightened eyes. Then I deliver my mail to the front door, say hello to Mrs. Ramsey, remind her to tie Damian back up and make my way out of the yard.

(He shrugs.)

FIONA. *(to FIST)* *That's* how you handle a big dog! Moron!

FIST. Who the hell goes around wearin' a whistle?

FIONA. Someone with more than half a brain in his head. Damn you, Fist. Six years of my life! Just thrown away. Thrown *away*! And I ain't never gonna get 'em back. How could you be so stupid?

FIST. And how could you be so cold? Not answering a guy's letters for six years. I called, I got Hubcap to write you letters and emails. And nothing! You didn't even give me the courtesy of tellin' me to go to hell, if that's how you felt!

FIONA. All right, if that's what you want. Go to hell!

FIST. So this is how it is?

FIONA. This is how it is!

FIST. Well, then, it's a good thing I came today, isn't it? Now we know where we stand. Goodbye, Fiona. If I never see your cold, cruel face again it'll be too soon!

FIONA. Goodbye, get out of here, don't let the door hit your sorry ass on the way out!

(He storms to the front door. MARVIN *watches the action with displeasure.)*

MARVIN. Oh brother.

(He lifts the whistle he is still holding and blows loud and long. FIST *and* FIONA *grab their ears.)*

All right! Now everybody just stop right where you are!

FIST & FIONA. What the frig!

FIONA. What are you doin', Marvin?!

MARVIN. Fiona, as much as I'd love to see him walk out of our lives forever, I can't let you end it this way.

FIONA. Why not?

FIST. Yeah, why the hell not?

MARVIN. Because Fist, she doesn't hate you, in spite of all the lousy things you've done over the years. In fact, she loves you. Yeah. Until me, you were the only person who ever really cared about her, even if it was in a highly unstable and often precarious way. And I could tell, even when she told me the bad stories about you, she missed you a lot.

*(*FIST *isn't sure how to respond to this unexpected news.)*

And Fiona, Fist didn't come here today to berate you OR to marry you. He came today to tell you that he's sorry about everything that has happened, and that he misses you and needs you as a friend. You two matter more to each other than you know, and it doesn't take a rocket scientist to see it. Fist is right, you do have ties that can't be broken. And I may be crazy, but my conscience will not allow me to stand here and watch you two just throw it all away!

(Enter SANDY.*)*

SANDY. Okay, I've got flowers. And after one more cup of coffee, I think our minister just might be able to stand up. Are we ready? Everything okay?

FIONA. Is that true, Fist? Did you come to apologize?

FIST. *(It is just dawning on him.)* Yeah, I guess I did.

(pause)

I messed up, Fiona, and I'm sorry about the bank job and the bad plan and you winding up in jail 'cause of me. I wish I could change it. But I can't. And I understand if you hate me, but I wish you wouldn't, 'cause I miss you, you know.

FIONA. *(touched)* You broke out of prison and came all the way to Las Vegas just to tell me that?

FIST. Yeah.

FIONA. You are such an *idiot*! Now you got no chance at parole. And who knows how many more years they're gonna *add* to your sentence! Oh, Fist...

(They stand looking at one another. She shakes her head and then walks towards him. They hug – two old friends who truly care about one another. After a moment, FIST*'s hands move south and he grabs her butt.)*

MARVIN. Hey! Hey!

FIONA. *(shoving* FIST *away)* What's wrong with you? And we were havin' such a nice moment.

FIST. I been in the slammer 6 ½ years, Fiona. Give a man a break.

FIONA. *(half shrugging, to* MARVIN*)* That is true.

FIST. So...you love Fiona enough that you're willin' to have me in your life?

MARVIN. Apparently so.

FIST. And you're sure this is the guy you wanna marry? Even with him bein' so puny?

FIONA. He's the biggest man I know.

FIST. Well, all right then. I guess you got my blessin'.

SANDY. I must have missed something. Does that mean we're back to you two getting married?

MARVIN. It sure does. Is the minister – ready?

SANDY. Let me check.

(She exits.)

FIONA. Oh, Marvin, we're really getting married!

(to **FIST***)*

And you're gonna stay and be our witness, right?

FIST. Yeah. I'll stay.

(We hear the sound of police car alarms.)

Damn!

*(***FIST** *runs to the door to look out.)*

POLICE. THIS IS THE LAS VEGAS POLICE. THE CHAPEL IS SURROUNDED. WE KNOW YOU'RE IN THERE, FIST. COME OUT NOW AND NO ONE GETS HURT.

FIONA. What should we do? Marvin?

MARVIN. Go out the back! Out the back!

(They push **FIST** *toward the backroom as* **SANDY** *enters.)*

SANDY. No good. They're in the alley, too.

FIONA. Is there any other way out?

SANDY. Just the front and the back. Sorry, kids.

FIONA. Oh, Fist. You never had no luck at all, did ya?

FIST. That's okay. Don't worry about it. I knew it was gonna work out this way. Hell, everybody in the whole joint knew where I was goin'. I just wish I coulda stayed and seen you twos married.

POLICE. PUT DOWN YOUR WEAPONS AND COME OUT, FIST. NO ONE HAS TO GET HURT HERE.

MARVIN. They think you're armed. That could buy us a few minutes. How fast can you marry us?

SANDY. Uh, well, see here's the thing...

(points to the back room)

We've had a setback. I didn't realize he was spiking the coffee I was giving him. I'm sorry.

MARVIN. Well, this is just great. Of all the wedding chapels we could have picked –

SANDY. Thank God you picked mine! This has been fabulous!

FIST. What's the problem?

MARVIN. We don't have a minister! And unless you're a minister, this isn't going to happen!

FIST. Well, ain't this your lucky day? Cause I am.

MARVIN. Am what?

FIST. A minister. I took a course in the joint. Got my reverend credentials.

FIONA. No way.

FIST. It was Hubcap's idea. Some scheme he was working on, he said we needed a minister to make it work, so… hell, I had the time.

MARVIN. Are you for real about this? You're really a –

FIST. Yep.

SANDY. Well then, kids, let's do this!

(*moving them into place*)

Bride, here. Groom, here. Reverend Fist, right here. Let's go, let's go!

MARVIN. This day is not exactly working out the way I planned.

FIONA. Are you disappointed?

MARVIN. How could I be? I'm marrying you.

FIST. (*brusquely*) All right, all right! Here we go. I hope I remember it all. Dearly beloved, we are gathered here today to join this woman, my beautiful Fiona who I love so much, and this man, who wouldn't be my first choice, but Fiona seems to love 'im. What are ya gonna do? Fiona, will you take this guy to be your husband? Will you love him and comfort him, honor and keep him, and forsaking all others, try to be a good wife to him and not bust his balls too much like you used to do to me?

FIONA. I will.

FIST. And you, will you take Fiona to be your wife? Will you love her and comfort her, honor and keep her, and forsaking all others, protect her from all the scumbags in the world and do a better job of lookin' out for her than I did?

MARVIN. I will.

POLICE. YOU'VE GOT TWO MINUTES, FIST. THEN WE'RE COMING IN.

SANDY. Go, go, go!

FIST. Okay, okay. Now, will you repeat your vows?

(with great speed; **FIONA** *is one beat behind him. It sounds like one big jumble of words.)*

FIST/FIONA. I, Fiona, take you to be my husband. To have and to hold, from this day forward, for better or worse, for richer or poorer, in sickness and in health, to love and to cherish for as long as we both shall live.

FIST. How 'bout you? You agree to all that?

MARVIN. *(speedily)* Yes, yes! For as long as we both shall live. Yes.

FIST. *(even faster)* Now the rings. C'mon, c'mon. Put 'em on. Put 'em on. Okay, okay, you said your vows, you put on the rings, so all I have do it pronounce you and you'll be married.

SANDY. Then do it!

FIST. By the power vested in me by the Department of Corrections of the state of Texas, I now pronounce you husband and wife.

(Before **MARVIN** *can kiss* **FIONA**, **FIST** *steps in to kiss her.)*

Sorry, but you've got the rest of your life to kiss her. You take care, baby.

POLICE. THIS IS THE POLICE. TIME'S UP. WE'RE COMING IN.

*(***FIST** *runs to the front door and yells out.)*

FIST. Hang on! I'm comin', I'm comin'!

FIONA. I'll write to you!

FIST. You'd better.

(He takes one last look at **FIONA**. *Then to* **MARVIN***)*

Hey – Marvin – kiss the bride already.

*(***FIST*** exits with his hands up.* **MARVIN** *and* **FIONA** *kiss.* **SANDY** *applauds.)*

SANDY. Congratulations! Congratulations!

(She hugs them both.)

Boy, you two are gonna have one great wedding story to tell your kids, huh?

MARVIN. And anybody else who wants to listen!

SANDY. Well, all you have to do now is sign the certificate and it's official.

MARVIN. You first, Mrs. Marvel.

FIONA. Thank you, Mr. Marvel.

(She signs.)

SANDY. And now you.

*(***MARVIN** *signs.)*

And that's it.

(She hands them the wedding certificate.)

I'd wish you kids good luck, but you don't need it.

MARVIN. Why not?

SANDY. Because I can tell – you've got the real thing.

MARVIN. I guess working in a wedding chapel you see it all the time, huh?

SANDY. Hardly ever, Marvin.

(hugs all around)

FIONA. Ohhh! Thank you, Sandy. We'll miss you!

MARVIN. Thanks, Sandy! Bye!

FIONA. Hey, Sandy!

(She tosses the bouquet over her shoulder, **SANDY** *catches it.)*

(as **MARVIN** *and* **FIONA** *exit)*

SANDY. Have a good life, kids!

(They exit. **SANDY** *stands alone in the chapel looking very pleased as the curtain closes.)*

Sandy & Ken: The Epilogue

(A year later. **SANDY** *is onstage looking lovely. On the desk is a bucket of champagne with several glasses surrounding it.)*

SANDY. Okay, I've got the champagne on ice. The caterer's setting up. I'm all dressed. The place looks great.

(calling to the back room)

Sweetie, how are you doing back there? Need help with your tie?

(We hear a muffled "no.")

Okay.

(to herself)

I can't believe I'm doing this again. We must be out of our minds. Oh well. The real question is, where are our guests?

(Enter **JOHN** *and* **BEV**.*)*

Ah!

JOHN. *(a bit subdued)* Hey Sandy. Sorry we're late.

SANDY. I was starting to get worried.

JOHN. Yeah, we should have been here a half hour ago.

BEV. Sandy! You look beautiful!

SANDY. Thank you. So do you. I love this. Where'd you get it?

BEV. A little shop out near Fremont Street. They've got great vintage clothes and jewelry. We should go sometime.

SANDY. I'd love to. You're becoming quite the Las Vegan, aren't you? John tells me you know this city better than he does now –

BEV. No.

SANDY. And that you've learned the chapel business like a pro. What do you think of it?

BEV. It's interesting, that's for sure.

SANDY. It gets even more interesting as you go. So, can you believe I'm really doing this?

BEV. Well, you always said the fifth time was going to be the charm.

SANDY. I know, but still, you two must think I'm crazy.

JOHN. *(still downbeat)* We think you're great. After all, if it wasn't for you, we would have never met and fallen in love. And I never would have…proposed.

SANDY. *(thrilled for them)* I knew it! I knew it was going to happen. Congratulations! I insist on marrying you in my chapel.

JOHN. Well, she hasn't answered me yet.

SANDY. *(awkward)* Oh. Oh. I see. Hmm. Dear. Well.

BEV. *(embarrassed)* John.

JOHN. Well, it has been a week. I mean, after a week don't you think a guy has a right to an answer?

SANDY. I really don't know. Why don't we have some champagne? I know we should probably wait until after the ceremony, but what the hell, huh?

(**SANDY** *pours several glasses.*)

BEV. Yes, please!

JOHN. It's just that if you love someone, it shouldn't be that tough a question, you know what I mean?

BEV. You are really embarrassing me.

JOHN. *(to BEV)* I don't know how else to get you to talk to me!

(to SANDY)

I don't know how else to get her to talk to me.

SANDY. Let's drink! To Sandy: always a bride, never a bridesmaid. To my wedding. The fifth one. Long may it wave.

*(They drink. It is awkward. **JOHN** sits.)*

BEV. So – where's the groom?

SANDY. Getting ready for the ceremony. I know it's crazy, but somehow I think this time's going to be different. Do you think that's possible?

BEV. For things to be different? I hope so. I mean, yes, of course. Of course.

(Enter **MARVIN** *and* **FIONA.** *)*

MARVIN. Hey Sandy. We made it!

SANDY. Oh my goodness! Look what just blew in from Wilber, Nebraska.

(They greet one another with hugs and hellos.)

John, Bev, this is Fiona and Marvin. I married them about, what, a year and a half ago?

MARVIN. Sixteen months, three days and two hours ago.

FIONA. Isn't he somethin'?

BEV. Hello. Nice to meet you.

JOHN. *(still sulking)* Yeah, hi.

SANDY. I think you're *both* something coming all this way for my wedding.

MARVIN. Are you kidding? We wouldn't have missed it. And this chapel, well, it's a real special place for Fiona and me, huh, angel?

FIONA. Oh yeah. It's just like I remembered it. That's where we told Sandy our whole story and that's where Fist nearly broke your hand, and that's where we were married as the police surrounded the building.

SANDY. Great memories, huh?

MARVIN & FIONA. *(sighing)* Yeah.

BEV. Was that a Cops & Robbers wedding theme?

SANDY. No, that was real life. Marvin and Fiona are one of my all-time greatest weddings. So, are you happy?

*(***MARVIN** *and* **FIONA** *look at one another and smile.)*

Yeah, you're happy. You ever hear from Fist?

MARVIN. *(His smile fading.)* Yeah, we hear from Fist.

SANDY. How's he doing?

FIONA. He's doing great! Marvin got him a good lawyer and guess what happened? They figured out that the cops at the bank never read him his rights, so they let him go! Can you believe it?

(**MARVIN** *shakes his head.*)

So he came to live with us, you know, just 'til he gets on his feet. What was that, a couple of weeks ago?

MARVIN. Three months, twelve days and seventeen hours.

FIONA. And guess what else?

SANDY. What?

FIONA. He's here now! He came with us!

SANDY. He's here?

MARVIN. Of course he's here. He's always here!

FIONA. He's just parking the car.

(*Enter* **FIST** *wearing a suit.*)

FIST. Hey, Chapel Lady! Congratulations! How about a hug for ol' Fist?

(*He lifts her up and spins her around.*)

SANDY. Oh my! Okay, okay, that's enough. And Fist, I think it's time you called me Sandy.

FIST. All right, Sandy! Wow. Things sure have changed since the last time we was here. I'm a free man.

SANDY. Yes, I heard.

FIST. And I'm a *better* man! And you know how come? You know how come? Because of this man right here.

(*He throws a crushing arm around* **MARVIN** *who winces.*)

I know he don't look like much, but this here is one great man. How many guys you know would get their wife's ex-boyfriend out of jail, and *then* let him move in with 'em, huh? And he has changed my life forever. Ain't that right, Fiona? Ain't I the best man I ever been since I moved in with youse?

FIONA. You sure are. He changed you just like he changed me.

(She puts her arm around him, so that **MARVIN** *is now sandwiched in between her and* **FIST**.*)*

SANDY. So you're just one big happy family, huh?

FIST. Yes! We are a *family*. And that's somethin' I ain't never had before.

(He wipes away a tear.)

FIONA. Oh, Fist.

MARVIN. *(extricating himself, with an obvious edge to his voice)* Okay, okay. One big happy family.

FIONA. Marvin, are you all right?

MARVIN. Of course. I'm terrific. How about some champagne?

(to **FIONA***)*

Can I get you a glass, angel?

FIST. Let me get that, Marvin.

MARVIN. No, I'll get it. She's my wife, and I can get her a glass of champagne!

FIST. Whoa, Marv. You seem a little on edge today.

FIONA. Yeah, you do, baby.

FIST. Anybody else think Marvin seems on edge? Sandy, what do you think? Don't Marvin seem on edge?

JOHN. Well, of course the man's on edge! You've been living in his house for three months!

MARVIN. And twelve days and seventeen hours!

JOHN. I'm surprised he's not standing on a ledge. The man would like his privacy – and his wife – back! It's not that hard to figure out.

FIST. And who are you?

JOHN. One very aggravated guy. I wouldn't mess with me right now if I were you.

FIST. Oh yeah? Tough guy, huh?

JOHN. Yeah, you want a piece of me? Come on, Finger, Hand, whatever your name is.

FIST. It's Fist, and I'd be glad to introduce ya to it.

(They start to circle, then push one another.)

JOHN. Come on over and get a piece of this, Marvin. You know you want to.

BEV. John! What are you doing?!

FIONA. Fist! For God's sake –

MARVIN. Look you guys, just stop –

(They bang into the champagne table.)

SANDY. Watch the champagne!

MARVIN. Oh, geez. Guys, guys! Guy!

*(**MARVIN** jumps in on the action trying to separate the two.)*

Stop it, come on, stop it!

(They don't stop. He pulls out his trusty whistle and blows. It is long and piercing. Everyone grabs their ears. The fight ends.)

SANDY. *(wincing)* Thank you, Marvin. I think.

*(to **JOHN** and **FIST**)*

What's the matter with you people?! This is my wedding day! And it's supposed to be special! Even if it is the fifth one!!

JOHN. Sorry, Sandy.

*(He looks at **BEV**.)*

I'm just a little stressed.

SANDY. And you! I thought you said you had changed?

FIST. I did. Didn't ya see my restraint? The old Fist woulda killed him by now.

SANDY. All right, all right. Let's just everybody calm down!

(She swigs a glass of champagne.)

*(Enter the **PRODUCER**, backing into the room, and holding a videocamera trained on the front door.*

PRODUCER. We are now entering Sandy's Chapel of Love. This is take one, and...*action!*

(Enter **VANESSA** *and* **BRYCE**. *They stride towards the camera pushing aside anyone in their way. They address the camera.)*

SANDY. What the hell?

VANESSA. Welcome friends. Today we'll be making plans for my upcoming wedding. Aren't weddings the most wonderful events, Bryce?

BRYCE. They sure are, Vanessa.

VANESSA. We've chosen a little chapel here in Las Vegas that specializes in celebrity weddings. Let's meet the proprietor.

(She grabs **SANDY** *and pulls her into the camera frame.)*

SANDY. What are you two doing here? Again?!

VANESSA. Again? No, you are mistaken. This is our first time here. Vanessa Wells!

BRYCE. And Bryce Cannon!

SANDY. Yes, I know who you are.

VANESSA. Well, of course you do.

BRYCE. The whole world knows who we are!

VANESSA. What you may not know is that Bryce and I are now the stars of our own hit reality show – a weekly docudrama chronicling the daily happenings and fascinating moments of our extraordinary lives. Today, we're making plans for my wedding to the Turkish ambassador, Ahmed Rashteegastan. Now, chapel proprietor, I would like you to take us through all of our options and show our viewers what a first class wedding looks like. I want this event to be fabulous! Shall we sit?

SANDY. No! We shall not sit. You can't just barge in here and take over the place. There's a wedding going on, for God's sake.

VANESSA. Oh. One of these little people here?

SANDY. If you must know, it's my wedding. I'm getting married. So just take your cameras out of here. And if you want to schedule filming another time, perhaps we can arrange something.

VANESSA. I'm sorry. That won't do. We're on deadline, you see.

BRYCE. Yes, we're on deadline.

(He taps his wrist watch.)

VANESSA. We need a completed segment by tonight. So why don't you just go ahead and finish up your little ceremony. And we'll just have a seat until you're done.

*(***VANESSA**, **BRYCE***, and ***PRODUCER*** *take a seat in the pews.)*

JOHN. *(approaching them)* I believe the lady asked you to leave.

MARVIN. Yeah, I heard her too.

FIST. So are you going to leave on your own, or do we have to –

SANDY. Guys, guys! That's okay. Let them stay. Fine. Whatever. They can film the wedding. You'll film my wedding – for free. Right?

(The **PRODUCER** *looks at* **VANESSA** *then nods his head.)*

Okay, so why don't we get started? Everyone take a seat and we'll get this thing going.

(Everyone sits. **SANDY** *stands before them at the altar.)*

Okay, well, we've gotten off to a little bit of a rocky start here, but maybe that's a good omen. Who knows? Anyway, I want to thank you all for coming to my wedding. Once you get to the fifth time, it gets a little embarrassing but I'm hoping – and believing – that this time is the last time. Marvin and Fiona: I asked you to come because you are by far the happiest couple I have ever married. You're an inspiration to couples everywhere. Well, maybe not at this particular moment since you seem to be having some issues, but normally speaking.

MARVIN. *(standing)* Oh, we're not having issues. Fiona and I couldn't be happier. She's an angel.

(He points to himself and **FIST**.*)*

We're having issues.

FIST. We are?

MARVIN. *Yes!*

FIST. I didn't know that.

MARVIN. That's why I'm *telling* you!

FIST. Is it what that guy was saying about you wantin' your privacy back?

MARVIN. *YES!*

FIST. Geez. I couldn't even tell. See, that's what so amazin' about this man.

> *(to* **PRODUCER***)*

> You should be filming *this* guy. Even when he's pissed off, he's still a nice guy. I got so much to learn from him.

MARVIN. Yeah, well, you're going to be doing it from your own apartment. You're moving out, Fist. OUT! I want Fiona all to myself and if I have to throw you out, I will. She's mine, okay? Mine, mine, mine!

FIONA. Marvin! You're being so – forceful.

> *(She likes it.)*

FIST. *(very willingly)* Okay, I'll move out.

MARVIN. You will?

FIST. Sure. Whatever you want. I can still come over though, right? And help you sort the mail, and work on my readin', and be a part of the family.

MARVIN. Yes, of course. Once a week.

FIST. I think I need at least twice a week. I got a long ways to go before I'll ever be as good as you.

MARVIN. Okay, twice a week. Then it's settled. Okay, Fiona?

FIONA. You're really somethin' when you're angry, aren't ya?

MARVIN. Well…

FIONA. I like it. Just wait 'til we get back to Wilber…

BRYCE. Where the hell is Wilber?

SANDY. It's in Nebraksa. That's where they live.

VANESSA. Nebraska? Dear god. You poor child.

(to **MARVIN**)

Why in the world would you drag her off to such a place?

FIONA. *(Her head snaps up.)* You gotta problem with Nebraska?

FIST. *(to **VANESSA**)* Uh oh. Now you've done it.

VANESSA. I'm not even sure where it is to tell you the truth.

FIONA. *(approaching **VANESSA** with major attitude)* You with your fine clothes and your camera crew and your Ken Doll boyfriend here.

VANESSA. He's not my boyfriend. He's gay as a mountain breeze.

FIONA. *(in her face)* I don't like you disrespectin' my husband and my home, *bitch.*

VANESSA. *(to **BRYCE**)* Did you hear what she just called me?

FIONA. Now you either say you're friggin' sorry or I'm gonna have to jack you up the way I did that snitch bitch in the big house. And it wasn't pretty!

VANESSA. *(getting up)* What is she saying? I don't understand any of these words.

BRYCE. *(getting up, cowering behind **VANESSA**)* I think she's planning to hurt you!

VANESSA. Well, protect me then, damn it! Protect me!

*(She and **BRYCE** struggle, each trying to get behind the other.)*

FIST. These two are pathetic.

SANDY. Just apologize and everything will be okay.

VANESSA. I'm sorry, I'm sorry! Apologies to you and your husband!

FIONA. And Wilber.

VANESSA. Of course, of course, apologies to Wilber. The Paris of the Midwest!

FIONA. All right then. That's better. Watch your 'tude.

*(She walks back to **MARVIN**.)*

VANESSA. My what?

*(to **PRODUCER** who has been eagerly filming)*

We're deleting all of that!

PRODUCER. No way! This is great stuff!

FIONA. I'm sorry, Marvin. And I was doin' so good for so long.

MARVIN. Don't apologize. I kind of like it when you get angry, too.

FIONA. You do?

MARVIN. Sure! What man doesn't love to have his woman stand up for him?

FIONA. Oh, Marvin.

MARVIN. Oh, Fiona.

(They look lovingly at each other.)

SANDY. Okay! Meanwhile back at Sandy's wedding –

FIONA & MARVIN. *(laughing)* Sorry, Sandy. Sorry.

(They sit.)

SANDY. John and Bev: I invited you because, well, John, you're one of my best friends. You've looked out for me for so many years, been there for me time and time again. I just love you. And Bev, you've made John so happy. Up until today, that is. Or maybe up until a week ago.

BRYCE. What happened a week ago?

VANESSA. Would you shut up?! These people are obviously unstable.

JOHN. *(standing)* I asked Bev to marry me. And it was really romantic. We had dinner at the Bellagio. Best hotel in the city, best table in the room. I even had a couple of violinists come over. And over a flaming Baked Alaska, I pulled out my grandmother's ring and asked her to be my wife. And she said... "Can I think about it?"

MARVIN. Ouch!

BRYCE. Damn!

FIST. Shit!

JOHN. Thank you!

BEV. Don't look at me that way, everybody. You don't understand. Of course I want to marry John. Nothing would make me happier than to be your wife.

JOHN. Are you saying you want to marry me?

BEV. The question is… do you want to marry me?

JOHN. Well, I asked you, didn't I?

BEV. I need for you to be sure. *Really sure.* Because I got left at this altar once. And I can't go through that again. Not with you.

JOHN. Is that what this is all about? *(She nods.)* Bev, I've waited a lot of years to find the right woman. And now I've found her, and she's you and yes, I am really, really, really, really, really, really, really, really, really, really sure.

BEV. In that case, yes!

(He takes a ring box from his jacket and places a ring on her finger. They hug and kiss.)

JOHN. It's official!

(The others applaud and say things like "congratulations," "that's wonderful," "how beautiful" etc.)

SANDY. Congratulations you two! I just love it when things work out.

(dabbing at eyes)

How's my makeup? Still good?

FIONA. You're fine.

SANDY. Now, what were we doing? Oh, right. Sandy was getting married!

(They all laugh.)

Where is my groom? Where is my minister? Come on guys, I'm not getting any younger out here!

(Several moments pass. The back door opens. Enter **LOU** *in a tuxedo.)*

VANESSA. Oh my god, it's that horrible little man. Don't tell me he's the minister?

SANDY. Of course not. He's the groom. Hi sweetie!

(SANDY and LOU embrace.)

You look wonderful!

LOU. No, *you* look wonderful! Hey everybody, can you believe how lucky I am? Look at my beautiful bride!

(noticing VANESSA and BRYCE)

Oh, look who it is! It's, it's –

(He can't come up with their names.)

VANESSA. *(flatly)* Vanessa Wells.

BRYCE. And Bryce Cannon.

LOU. Right, right. Thanks for coming.

(to the others)

These two have been down on their luck for a long time.

(an attempted aside)

She's a lush and he's a fruit.

VANESSA. We can hear you.

LOU. How about we get this show on the road, huh? I've got a honeymoon to get started.

SANDY. Well, all we need now is the minister. Ken! Ken, we're ready! John, would you go get him?

(JOHN goes go the back room.)

He promised me he'd be okay to do this. And believe it or not, we all became good friends, me, Lou and Ken. It just seemed so natural to ask him.

(Enter JOHN.)

Well?

JOHN. Sorry, Sandy. Ken's sick. You know what I mean?

SANDY. Yeah, I know what you mean. Feel like performing a wedding?

JOHN. I would be honored to.

> *(They all take their places.)*

> Dearly beloved, we are gathered here today to join this man and this woman –

SANDY. Wait, wait, wait –

LOU. What's wrong? You're not changing your mind, are you?

SANDY. No! I just thought, what the hell, as long as John's doing the ceremony, why don't we get married by Elvis?

JOHN. I don't have my costume.

SANDY. That's okay. What do you think, Lou?

LOU. I love it! Marry us, Elvis!

JOHN. Well, all right. I'm never one to turn down a gig as the King! Here we go.

> *(removing his jacket, tie, putting on sun glasses, and grabbing the microphone)*

> Ladies and gentlemen, live from Las Vegas it's show time! Welcome to the wedding of two very special kids in love: Sandy and Lou. We're going to celebrate your special day and your special union – Elvis style!

> *(He sings a love song as the King. The rest of the group joins in as the lights go down. The actors clear the stage. Lights back up.* **KEN** *enters wearing minister collar. He looks around. Where is everybody? He spies the champagne, staggers across the stage and grabs a bottle.)*

KEN. *(as he exits)* Thank you. Thank you very much.

> *(Lights down.)*

THE COOLEY GIRLS

Brad Stephens

Dramatic Comedy / 1m, 5f

Three sisters, Rose, Brenda and Harriet Cooley, have been separated since childhood. Now forty years later, one of the sisters, Rose, decides to find her lost siblings and reunite the 'girls'. All of them have secrets to hide, but it is curiosity that finally brings them together for their unexpected reunion. Only when Harriet is forced to admit her most damning secret does this hard-bitten and humorous play resolve once and for all the bond each shares with the other. Perfect for community stages.

OTHER TITLES AVAILABLE FROM BAKER'S PLAYS

SEE YOU IN BELLS

Edie Claire

Comedy / 6m, 6f, 2 teen girls, 1 teen boy, and a good-natured minister / A church sanctuary

The mother of the bride has every reason to panic. Three generations of Bower family weddings—three inexplicable disasters. Now, with the church building falling down, half the wedding party AWOL, and the bride's sisters still fighting over what happened at the last family wedding, daughter Jenna's nuptials seem hopelessly doomed. But peacemaking brother Brian is determined to end the sisters' feud—and the family curse. All he needs is to stage a rip-roaring intervention…and pray it turns divine!

OTHER TITLES AVAILABLE FROM BAKER'S PLAYS

KEEPSAKES

Pat Cook

Drama / 4m, 6f / Interior

Ever look at a family portrait and wonder what those people, posed and smiling, are really like? This family portrait shows you the inner workings of the Rogers family – how they deal with everyday things, how they deal with both happy and sad events which effect each and every one of them. These funny, poignant and all-too-human characters go through life the best way they know how.

Austin does his best to keep the house running smoothly, unless he has to take Pawpaw's trunk out of the basement. Mary Jo is outwardly pleased when son Mitchell gets engaged to Tish but explains "They're too young!" Her sister, Brenda, helps out by saying "Not any younger than you were when you got married." Brenda's husband, Dale, has his own advice for young Mitchell – "Marriage consists in large part of just giving up!" And Pawpaw keeps hearing voices and seeing people who aren't there.

The very fabric of the family unit meets its ultimate challenge when Brenda and Dale have to move in with them. Daughter Jan has to put up with a whiney dog, Mitchell and Tish can't seem to find time to talk about their upcoming marriage and everyone is bunking up with everyone else, leaving the men to sleep on the couch – any of this sound familiar? Brought to you by the same author of *Good Help is So Hard to Murder.*

Lightning Source UK Ltd.
Milton Keynes UK
UKHW020610290722
406556UK00008B/469

9 780874 407389